Wildness in a Small Place

A portion of the purchase price of this book supports environmental education projects at the Latodami Environmental Education Center

Wildness in a Small Place

Randy Minnich

Illustrations by:

Erin Sloane, Joe Stavish, and Caity Stone

The following poems have been published previously: "Acorns" in The Unitarian
Universalist Poets, December, 1995, "Balance" in The Nature Observer News,
December, 2002, and "Dogwood Blossoms" in Pudding, vol. 33, April, 1997.

Front cover photograph: Kurt Gasparik
Book design and back cover photograph: Cheryl Neuendorffer

First Edition
Printed in the United States of America

Contents

List of Poems

Illustrations

Forward

This journal has been, for me, a journey of discovery. Not discovery in the grand sense of, say, Shackleton's Antarctic adventure, of course. That's only daydream material for most of us. Rather, this journal is of discovery on a scale accessible to all of us: just walks in a local nature area to learn what I can of the local flora and fauna. But if I could leave just one thought with you, it would be that these special, often overlooked places hold more to learn, love, and wonder about than any of us could absorb in a lifetime.

I believe that keeping a journal helps us to absorb more than we otherwise would. It pushes us to observe more closely and contemplate what we've seen. So, I hope that this journal will encourage you to begin your own. We've tried to leave white spaces here and there for you to fill, if you will. I'd be delighted if you would take the book to the woods and write in it what you see. I'd be honored if you mingle your observations with mine. I'd love to see these same places through your eyes.

It is said that anyone who tries to identify birds (or plants or anything else) will surely misidentify them sometimes. That applies to experts, as well as to the rest of us. I have striven for accuracy, of course, but please remember that I'm like you: a curious amateur, learning as I go. I have a long shelf of field guides and some knowledgeable friends. You'll find, usually in italics, explanations that came to me later. Also, some early readers who aren't yet birders asked for details that birders take for granted. You'll find many of those details in italics, as well. If you're a birder, just remember that we all start somewhere, pass over what you already know so well, and think of the comradeships in binocular-toting that may be forming.

You'll find names of birds, too—lots of them, indeed, too many of them, said two non-birding friends who served as first readers. These are people whose opinions I take very seriously—one is my wife, Claudia! So I considered changes. But then I remembered my first impression of Robert Pyle's <u>Chasing Monarchs</u>. I thought it an excruciatingly detailed account of a crackpot journey from British Colombia to Texas, following a trail of flight paths of passing Monarchs. There were far too many butterfly names—with every turn of the page, still more butterfly names! I thought him, in those first pages, a pretentious, half-mad stuffed-shirt professor, but as the miles on his dusty old Honda rolled on and Rocky Mountain vistas opened before him, my mind began to open, too. By the time the young English hikers caught him skinny-dipping in the Colorado, I'd learned a great deal about nature, met yet another fascinating person, and realized another principle to live by. In this specific case, it is: if I have the cheek to peer out at the world through the eyes of an entomologist, I had better expect to see a lot of bugs—many wearing name tags. When Bob Pyle arises, he sees the state of the world—the daily news, to a naturalist—written in butterflies and beetles.

I bought a field guide to butterflies so I could see the world a little more as he does. And now, for example, *Nathalis iole irene* doesn't just conjure memories of Caesar's interminable march through the dark forests of Latin classes right after lunch. It also calls forth the dainty sulfur butterfly, a fragile-looking little butterfly, about the size of a fingerprint, with black spots on its yellow wings. Most flutter all year among the daisies of Mexico, but some pioneer spirits forge north on diaphanous wings to colonize the Pacific Northwest for a summer. There's a lot wrapped up in those butterfly names.

The bird names stay in.

You'll also find poetry and drawings. There are moments that escape prose. There are thoughts that escape analysis. The poems are my responses to these. They reach back several years and some recall other places, but I think they capture some of those escapees. Three artist friends have added drawings from the nature center to replace a thousand or so of my futile words.

We should stop talking about the woods and go there. But those woods would have been mute were it not for you who were determined that they should have a voice. Let me thank you before we march off.

Thanks to Meg Scanlon, Interpretive Naturalist for Latodami, to my editors, Molly Lundquist and Joan Bauer, to the members of the Squirrel Hill Poetry Workshop for very helpful criticism, to Cheryl and Tom Neuendorffer for turning the manuscript into a book and for the back cover photograph, to Kurt Gasparik for the front cover photograph, to my three artists, Joe Stavish, Caity Stone, and Erin Sloane, to Jose Taracido of California University of Pennsylvania, and to Claudia Minnich for support, encouragement, and advice.

And thanks also to those who have guided and enlightened me without knowing—the authors of some very good books.

Living on the Wind, Scott Weidensaul, North Point Press, New York, 1999
Gatherings of Angels: Migrating Birds and Their Ecology, edited by Kenneth P. Able, Cornell University Press, Ithaca, NY, 1999
The Sibley Guide to Bird Life and Behavior, David Allen Sibley, Alfred A. Knopf, NY, 2001
The Immense Journey, Loren Eiseley, Random House, New York and Toronto, 1957
Chasing Monarchs, Robert Pyle, Houghton Mifflin Company, New York and Boston, 1999.

Finally, three of the poems have been published previously: "Acorns" in The Unitarian Universalist Poets, December, 1995, "Balance" in The Nature Observer News, December, 2002, and "Dogwood Blossoms" in Pudding, vol. 33, April, 1997.

Now to the woods.

Introduction

I retired in mid-September, 2001, at the age of 59. That surprised many of my colleagues; it still surprises me at times. The reasons weren't simple, of course, but the usual culprits weren't among them. I liked the job, the people, and the company. If blame for my decision could be laid on anyone, it would be upon John Denver. You see, outside my office window, just a glance above my computer screen, lay a meadow, and beyond that, a woods. And through that space on the other side of the pane, warblers, robins, monarch butterflies— indeed, much of Noah's host—passed in their respective seasons. As season after season passed, too, John Denver's song, "I Guess He'd Rather Be In Colorado" tapped gently, then ever more insistently on my mind as seasons rolled into years and years into decades:

> "In the end, up in his office,
> In the end, a quiet cough is
> All he has to show he lived in New York City".

Not that there is special magic in Colorado. If there is magic for me, it's been in all the woods and meadows and waters I've known. I'm drawn to all such places. If this is a spell, then it was cast by wood sprites, or brown-eyed does. Perhaps they're the same.

Of course, I've answered their calls all my life, as we all do, to the lengths that the threads of our other loves allow. But these little forays have seemed like snippets and sound-bites. I have wanted to see one whole year pass, to be out in it as it passes. I've wanted to hear the sermon whole, not at one sitting, of course, but at least from the same pew.

Retirement offered me time, but where would I set my pew? I live, and likely will live, surrounded by city. Indeed, as the oak woods tumble to the roars of chain saws and bulldozers, and the raw-mud mounds that were our hills are pushed into the valleys, I am continually more surrounded by city. Nonetheless, the answer was simple. A long-departed uncle taught me, years ago, that there is wildness and beauty all around, even in small places, if you look. The key is to appreciate what you have, and leave it better. He walked the walk: born to a poor family by a small muddy stream in rural western Ohio and largely self-educated, he first learned the river with a fishing rod in his hand, then organized conservation groups, agitated around the county, wrote to, then talked with, the governor. The Stillwater is now an Ohio Scenic River.

But the Stillwater runs 300 miles from here, and the mountains and forests of western Pennsylvania aren't close enough for casual visits. Fortunately, my uncle's kindred spirits set aside, long before my time or even his, a series of parks in Allegheny County. North Park is ten minutes from my house.

North Park is a 3,000 acre county park in Pittsburgh's northern suburbs. Most of it, especially in the valley, is heavily used, well-known, and loved by thousands. There are athletic fields, jogging paths, picnic areas—the full array of facilities that municipal parks offer. That part of the park is alive with people, always active and often boisterous. There, it's easy to forget that much of this land was once farm and woodland—and much quieter.

But the encircling hills remember that past, albeit dimly. Rusted, broken fence lines run at odd angles through groves of huge old hardwoods and across hillsides covered by younger second growth, no longer denying passage nor delineating anything to anyone. A few old gravestones stand on a wooded hill, overlooking the valley. Hikers, birdwatchers, dog-walkers know of an old windmill, domed root cellars, and other remnants of farm life. Those who pause to look and listen know also of the abundance of wildlife.

I have placed my pew among those hills.

Though the sermon will last a year, I do already know the church. I've been walking in those woods for years, sporadically. Many of the "snippets and sound-bites" have been gifts from such walks, especially in an area near Walter's Road. There, a little stream has carved a small valley. It's a very minor wilderness, overbrowsed by deer and covered with only the early trees of the succession. But it has the stream, a marshy area, an upland hillside, and both an old oak woods and a golf course nearby. It seems like a good place for a pew.

Before I sit down, I can guess a couple of the themes. I will be in an encapsulated wildness; such areas seem likely to be our legacy. I'm tempted to call it a shrinking wildness, but if my backyard and birdfeeder are indicators, there are many who are quite wild and yet doing very well in the interstices of our urban sprawl. I expect this to be a journey that uncovers wonder and beauty in rather ordinary places.

I also expect it to be a journey of discovery. I've lived most of my life in a lab. Quite likely, I have no idea how little I know about the natural world.

Other themes will probably emerge. But whatever they may be, if you choose to come with me and we both emerge on the other side with a greater sense of humility and wonder, it will have been a very good year.

To the Woods

September 27

So let us start the year today in the woods by Walters Road. The morning is cold (about 50°F) and windy, with rain predicted. None has fallen yet, but the air is damp. Occasionally, the sun breaks through.

I enter the woods to the sounds of blue jays, crows, and dump trucks. The birds appear to be mobbing a hawk or owl; the trucks are laboring up the hill to the landfill in the middle of North Park. A landfill in a park seems like an oxymoron at best, an obscenity at worst. But the birds are going about their business, so I guess I'll go about mine.

The hillside between the road and the stream is very active. A flock of starlings flies over in synchronized ranks. Robins seem to be everywhere: flitting through the trees, searching in the leaves and grasses. Many of the usual birds one sees all year are around me, too: a red-bellied woodpecker, a titmouse (scolding me), chickadees, a Carolina wren in the distance. A squirrel and a chipmunk rustle about. The crows finally flush the red-tailed hawk they've been pestering. White snakeroot is scattered across the hillside; horseweeds are tattered and brittle along the stream. The leaves on the trees are still green and not at all ready to fall.

I had hoped to see some sign of migration in progress. The annual flow of rivers of birds, both northward and southward, is deeply moving to me. I'm simply awestruck by the fact of it: whole species, moved by a voice from deep within, spread small wings, leap onto the wind and, risking everything, row into the night. Migration holds religious significance for me. As hundreds of millions of other humans find a sense of oneness with something infinitely larger through the pageantry of religious ceremony, so I find it in this annual, monumental movement of life. In spring, the tide rushing to the northern breeding grounds fills me with the joy of return and rebirth. Now, in autumn, as the tide ebbs southward I am torn between loss and loveliness. Autumn is so mixed. It is, of course, a time of ripeness and fulfillment. But, too, the melancholy of the earth's inexorable march toward dark and desolate days seeps through the ecstasy of crimson trees framed by cerulean skies. For autumn is a grand finale—like the last booming crescendo of Fourth of July fireworks—with the emptiness of endings at the core.

And, in some places, the migrations can be as dramatic as fireworks. Along the Allegheny Escarpment, on the big inland lakes, on peninsulas that focus the flights across the Great Lakes, the tides of migration are like a tidal bore: a current of birds sweeping through. Sometimes the flow itself is obvious, sometimes not. Soaring birds fly during the day, since they ride thermal air

17

currents generated by the sun. Birders flock to mountain ridges to watch lines of eagles, hawks, and vultures float by. But most birds fly at night so they can rest and find food by daylight. Few people see those long, dark flights. Flocks do show up on coastal radar as swirls on a fluorescent screen. Mostly, though, the migrants simply appear—as hundreds of gabbling water birds on the lake, a beach swarming with stilt-legged shorebirds, or trees aflutter with small yellow birds. They weren't there yesterday; tomorrow, they'll be gone.

Such moments at the focal points of migration can be frantic. Torn and tattered pages in field manuals attest to that. I know one experienced birder who, surrounded by hundreds of migrant warblers, many surely of species not yet on his life list, simply gave up on identification and watched, grinning.

Most of us, however, live where the flow is more diffuse. North Park is like that. The birds pass through, but you have to be looking to see them. The black angles of a cormorant will appear on a bare branch overlooking North Park Lake. A northern duck will paddle among the resident geese. Or the pines are suddenly still—the grackles have left.

So, today, I'm looking for whatever news of the migration the woods may offer. I imagined that the warblers had already gone, but thought I might see a flock of some later migrant. But here is a warbler! It's just a yellow underside, brown above, and quickly gone, but it is a warbler. As I walk up the hill toward the landfill, there, in a locust tree, is a gray-cheeked thrush! I haven't seen one of them since Alaska, two years ago. There should be more, so I sit under a tree for quite a while, watching. I don't see any, and finally the trucks and bulldozers get to me.

As an afterthought, I decide to check out the Latodami Nature Area on Brown Road. Though I've driven past it, I've never hiked there.

The parking area is beside an old barn that overlooks a small pond and marshy outflow. The surrounding hills are wooded. The woods on one hill across the road appear to be fairly young, as though that hillside had been farmed and is now in the early succession of meadow to woodland. Mature oaks and hickories cover an adjacent hill. A little stream flows between the two hills and into the pond. This diversity of habitats seems very promising. I usually see the most wildlife at the boundaries of habitats: edges of woods, along streams, beside ponds and marshes.

Indeed, Latodami seems even livelier than the area around Walters Road. Again, there are birds that I wouldn't expect this late in the year: two wood ducks, two phoebes, at least one towhee. And regulars: mallards, song sparrows, two red-tailed hawks soaring very high, lots of jays, another red-bellied woodpecker. A deer snorts at me from somewhere up the hillside. I really like this place. Perhaps I'll move my pew.

October

Names

As the sun's golden slant
lies ever more recumbent
on the ridge,
tiny flowers glow whiter
on the darkening forest floor.

> *Small fuzzy heads in rounded clusters;*
> *opposite, heart-shaped leaves...*
> *I used to know their name.*
> *Compositae...something.*

As the bumblebee lands heavily
on each pale bloom along
the drunken little farmer's zigzag path,
the flower bows gratefully
and patiently awaits the milker.
Upside down, he fumbles
among the fragile little nipples.

> *I ought to look it up again,*
> *but since it fled before,*
> *perhaps I'll simply leave it.*
> *One more unnamed wonder.*

23

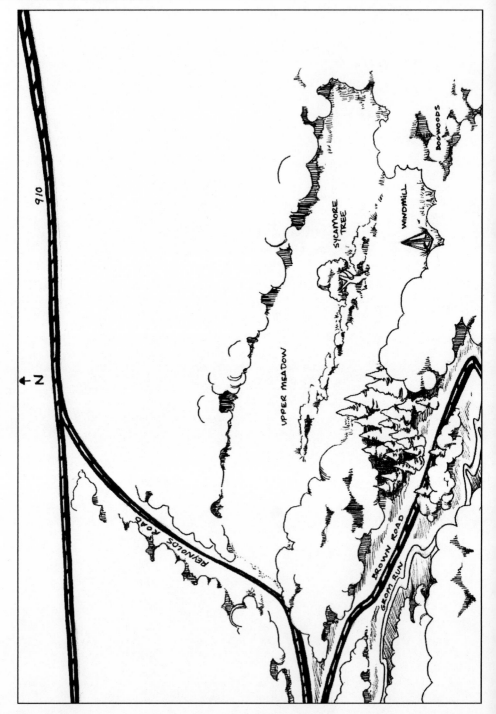

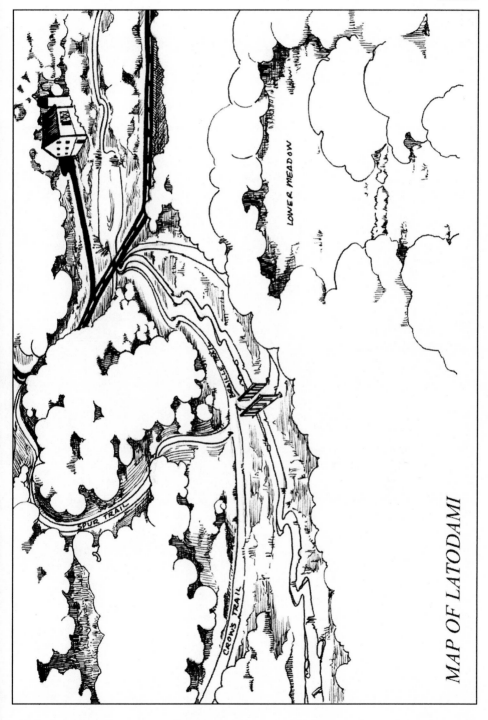

October 3

On a warm, cloudless morning, I've come to the pond and marshy area at the nature center on Brown Road. It seems unlikely that I'll want to leave.

As I approach the pond, six mallards paddle quickly to the opposite side. Breezes ruffle the water, and large green-striped dragonflies patrol their domains like little helicopters, hovering, then darting for something. Their wings glisten in the sun. Phoebes perch on bare branches of overhanging trees. They're a study in alertness, flicking their tails as they peer this way and that through round black eyes. Suddenly, one swoops down upon a bug, then loops back to its post. As I watch, bug after bug disappears down those graceful gullets. Surely, they're fattening up for the flight to the Gulf. Their small upright silhouettes against the bright yellow-green leaves of the trees on the hillside add drama to their hunt. But while migration seems momentous to me, birds seem to be rather matter-of-fact about most things.

"Most things" don't include the appearance of a hawk. In the distance, jays and crows had been mobbing a red-tail. Now the hawk slips through the clearing in usual hawk fashion: by the time I realize it's there, it isn't. Its entourage is more leisurely, and much louder.

"Mobbing" is a good description, but the word does have a precise meaning in ornithology: the harassment of a predator or kleptoparasite by one or more individuals from one or more species of birds. When mobbing, the birds chase, dive at, and scream alarm calls at the predator, usually until it leaves their territory. The motives for mobbing are probably complex. Surely, driving a predator away from a nest is one motive, but the predator is usually too large for the birds to hurt much. Distraction is probably just as important. Another motive is thought to be education of the young, and there are probably others, for often the cat, owl, or whatever is of no immediate danger to the mobbing birds. Maybe they just enjoy venting. I've never seen a bird, predator or otherwise, hurt during mobbing. Also, I've never seen a sharp-shinned hawk mobbed— although the large hawks can't catch a small bird on the wing, sharp-shinned hawks can. That's how they make their living.

The ducks have decided that I'm harmless and have drifted back to their hideaway under an overhanging maple tree. They bathe and nap a few feet from me.

I leave them dabbling quietly and walk downstream into the marsh. There, a warbler-like bird hunts insects up the side of a tree and upside down under leaves. At first, I identify it as a female chestnut-sided warbler, but from the wing fluttering, I think it must be a female ruby-crowned kinglet. Not a migrant, but usually shy and briefly seen. This one is neither. Although I stare at her insolently through big black binoculars, she finishes a thorough search through a rock elm, then starts on a poison ivy-covered willow.

The red of the ivy against the green and yellow of the trees, bees on purple asters and white snakeroot, crickets in the background—such scenes were the stuff of my Latin-class daydreams, yet now my eyelids droop from pure placidity. They snap open again when a pair of downy woodpeckers alight in the poison ivy. The woodpeckers are surprisingly possessive; when a chickadee arrives, they chase it away. What's wonderful about poison ivy? On the pond, pairs of red dragonflies, attached head-to-tail, dance what must be a mating ritual: over the water to dunk the tail of the back dragonfly into the water, then to a wet, moss-covered log to rap the tail against the log, then back to the water. They repeat this with the monotonous persistence of a stamping machine. My eyes drift out of focus. My jaw goes slack. Perhaps this is the punishment for watching someone else's sex life.

(*I've since learned that this is an egg-laying process called contact guarding, and the dragonflies were some species of skimmers. For these dragonflies, the competition to procreate isn't over even after mating has occurred. The males are equipped to scoop competitive sperm out of the female and then deposit their own. So, to make sure his sperm isn't removed, the male tows the female around, picks the egg-laying site, and helps her lay the eggs.*)

A kingfisher rattles by. A chipmunk almost walks over my foot, then is deeply offended when I move. It vanishes behind a tree, calling me all the names it knows. A white-throated sparrow passes through, followed a bit later by a catbird. I had thought I heard the catbird earlier, but the blue jays were being so creative that I wasn't sure. A thrush flies from the bushes into the rock elm. It seems pretty offended, too: it sits on a branch, scolding and all fluffed up. I'm not sure which thrush it is. I know the thrushes' songs, but can't make anything out of all this chatter. It's probably a veery, since it isn't doing the tail-flicking of a hermit thrush, and the area is right for it. Perhaps, in May, he'll come back and sing—and I intend to be here to listen.

We both hope to be here in May, of course, but before that day, he must fly to Central America and back, find his forest there intact, avoid falling, exhausted, into the Gulf of Mexico, evade the small hawks that "escort" the flights of small birds, dodge tall antennae and glass-walled buildings and, through some miracle of navigation, find Latodami among the subdivisions. My way may be difficult, too. Who knows? No matter. I stand in awe of the paths of the veery and the phoebe. Their journeys are so long and dangerous, and they are so small and vulnerable. To match their feat, we would have to walk the Oregon Trail twice a year, empty-handed and surrounded by enemies.

I've noticed that I worry about others as they leave on long trips, but am quite nonchalant as I dash off on trips of my own. I suppose it's the same with the birds; the veery certainly seemed well-fed and feisty. Birds are a lot tougher than they look. To me, though, in autumn, the migrants wear an aura of heroism.

October 9

On this sunny, but cool morning, the air at Latodami rings with screams and shouts as several classes of children tour the paths. The ducks are in the middle of the pond. At first, I look for a place to hide, too. With all this racket, I doubt that I'll see much non-human wildlife. But the kids are friendly and curious; they ask what I see through my binoculars before they're shepherded onward by the adults. I'm happy they're seeing this, actually, and they pass swiftly by, like youth itself, leaving only small footprints in the mud.

As water seeps into those little impressions, the area's natural owners drift back to their daily routines: ducks to dabble at the edge of the pond, white-throated sparrows to scratch beneath the bushes, chickadees to probe among the branches. Of the usual pond life, only the dragonflies are missing. Perhaps 50° is too low for them. But the phoebes haven't left, so some insects must still be active.

Kinglets are supposed to be reclusive. I have seen few in my lifetime, and those usually fleetingly. But the one I saw in the marsh last week is in the same bushes today. Busy again with her bug-hunting, she gives me time to notice her wing-bars, her nervous wing-flicking, her acrobatics among the high twigs. I watch her till the jays chase a hawk by. Sometimes, identifying a bird is a casual business: looking at the bird through binoculars, looking down at the field guide or drawing on a pad, looking back up at the bird… At other times, it's matching a half-remembered shape with the afterimage from a swift flight across your retina. So it was with this hawk: a blur of wings, a very long tail disappearing into the trees, and blue jays tagging along, screeching. It was probably a northern harrier, but I can't be sure.

And summer, too, has slipped away. The woods look older than they did last week: more golden and leaner. Leaves clatter down through the branches at every breath of a breeze. Most of the apples have fallen. The brook is full of them. A few seem to have been gnawed by hornets and wasps, but most are whole.

There is so much to see, and I know so little. I'd love to know more about the plants around me. The "purple asters" from last week appear to be New York asters (alternate, long, thin, pointed, toothless leaves with little leaflet pairs at the base of each leaf; multiple purple petals around a yellow center). There are patches of red-stalked brambles (alternate compound leaflets, seven per stalk, fine teeth, little red berries on stalks, but in bunches). They must be a type of "prickly bramble," maybe a type of rose. A red-stemmed bush has opposite, toothless leaves about 3 1/2 " long. I suspect that it's a dogwood, maybe red-osier. Finally, a 15' shrub with multiple, smooth gray stalks, alternate leaves about 2" long and silver underneath, and reddish berries with gray speckles. My best guess is tall deerberry. But my real conclusion is that learning about the local shrubbery will teach me a lot about detailed observation and the need to take good notes with drawings. Sounds like fun, but my timing isn't good: the leaves are falling.

The "tall deerberry" is, in fact, autumn olive. This is an alien, but has been introduced because it grows quickly in poor soil, slows erosion, and is a good source of food and cover for wildlife. It even fixes nitrogen from the air, like a legume. Unfortunately, it's so successful that it crowds out other shrubs and hinders the reintroduction of a more diverse culture of native plants. Some naturalists are beginning to regret its introduction.

By early afternoon, the temperature is in the sixties. The sky is deep blue. Into that blue sky, a gust flings a thousand yellow willow leaves, like a handful of golden confetti that will not, can not, fall to earth, but rise glittering hundreds of feet into the sky. They flicker out of sight, still climbing. And when they have passed, a red-tailed hawk takes their place, circling white against the blue.

A monarch butterfly flies over, about 50' up and headed west. I wish it well. It's late. Frost is expected tonight, so it will have to get south of the freeze. If bird migrations are miraculous, what can I say about the butterfly's?

Other insects have become active, too. The dragonflies now stalk the surface of the pond. Several cabbage-white butterflies dance over the meadow to a syncopated ditty beyond my hearing. And, as I approach my car, an anglewing butterfly, either a question mark or hop merchant, sits beside the road. I wasn't aware, but both those species migrate, too.

Other migrants haven't left yet, either: a turkey vulture and a catbird. The white-throated sparrow is a migrant too, though it's probably on the southern end of its journey. As I leave, chickadees and cardinals are flitting about in the poison ivy. There's no accounting for taste.

October 17

Monet might have painted the trees around the pond: shimmering green and yellow splashes in golden sunlight. Frayed little clouds scoot hastily across the blue canvas toward Philadelphia. The morning is cool, probably in the high forties.

As I settle myself in the ridges and folds of an ancient willow, a flock of sleek little brown-streaked birds sweep in to inspect the tree. They have to be yellow-rumped warblers, but their autumn colors leave me unsure. They flit up, down, and upside down through the tree, almost landing on me a couple of times, but none will turn its back to me. I can't watch warblers without laughing; perhaps they feel the same about me. At last one flashes its yellow rump at me so I'll put the binoculars down. With all the berry bushes in the area, they may stay all winter.

Nine mallards float near the shore, soaking up the sunshine when they aren't splashing about like a fat man in a bathtub. In the background, a red-bellied woodpecker, cardinals, crows, and blue jays sing rustic background music for the fat man's bath.

The poison ivy's leaves are far fewer, and the remnants are yellow or withered brown scraps. But the berries hang in fat waxy white clusters. Several white-throated sparrows and the warblers gorge themselves on little pearls that would surely send me gagging to my grave. At the rate they're going, I wonder how far into the winter the berries will last.

In the marsh, I look again at the "prickly brambles" from last week. The red berries contain several white seeds inside, so I guess they must be rose hips. Apparently, they aren't a choice food for wildlife. I wonder who will eat them and if they'll last longer than the poison ivy berries.

In the drier, open field, birds and butterflies are becoming very active as the day warms. Bluebirds and blue jays startle me with their fluorescent blueness against the autumn browns and yellows. Cabbage white butterflies and some sulfur species flutter all around. Warm sunshine, blue sky, little puffs of occasional breezes—this would be the artist's vision of tranquility—if s/he were deaf. For in one tall tree, every bird in the world is exuberantly whistling, squawking, and screeching all possible bird sounds—in triplicate. It has to be a mockingbird. Sounds like several. He even mimics a jay, which seems redundant. Finally, he takes a break to pull apart an old tent caterpillar mass at the top of the tree. I'm surprised and delighted to see him this late in the year. I hope he's enjoying his performance as much as I am.

There are at least five accomplished mimics at Latodami: mockingbirds, brown thrashers, catbirds, blue jays, and starlings. They're seldom hard to identify. Mockingbirds amuse me the most. When it seems like a mass escape from the Aviary is passing through a single tree, three birds per species, there's a mockingbird in that tree. Mockingbirds are immoderate. Brown thrashers can be creative, too, but sing their phrases in pairs. Catbirds sing each phrase once, but in strings of sound that can border on madness with an occasional "pretty bird" or "meow" stuck in, perhaps to help the bird keep his place. Jays seem to have a mean streak. They have their own calls, ranging from the raucous to the bell-like and beautiful, but seem to find special enjoyment from deception and disruption—the shriek of a hawk in a quiet woods, for example. Starlings are gifted, too, but I haven't heard them often.

At the edge of the meadow, a mass of vines climbs a large sassafras tree. American bittersweet, I think. (*More likely, it's Asian bittersweet, another aggressive invasive that is far too successful.*) The orange berries open to reveal several red seeds inside. It ought to be the subject of some still-life painting. As I sit blinking in the sun, a flock of cedar waxwings and a savannah sparrow land, not in the bittersweet, but in some viburnum in the tangle. Goldfinches sway upside down from goldenrod and snakeroot heads. The birds—even the mockingbird—seem too busy to sing, so the morning has grown still and warm. The sun lies heavily on my eyelids.

But the world calls, so I shake free from the weight of peacefulness and head homeward. Not alone, though. I carry much of next year's meadow on my coat: burs, sticktights, and an array of other hooked seeds. "Fair enough," I say. "Come along."

October 23

Today, I am walking the Braille Trail west of Brown Road. The main trail is a loop: it goes up one side of a little stream, then circles to come down the other side. Its head is a confluence of habitats: the valley stream, mature oak and hickory on one hillside, a tangle of barberries, bittersweet, and viburnum on the other, and the cattail marsh the stream flows into. It's the sort of place where one expects to see wildlife. And there, in the barberries, are towhees and white-throated sparrows. A red squirrel, a fox squirrel, and several chipmunks scratch and scramble under the barberries and up the small second-growth trees. A blue jay drinks from the stream. And leaping from a small branch for dangling bittersweet berries is that thrush I still can't name. It doesn't seem to flick its tail, which says it's a veery, but it's so late that it must be a hermit thrush. In the spring, it will sing its name to me, but for now, it's a project.

The morning is warm for October. The temperature is already 70°. The sky has a thin stratus cloud cover. The wind is gusty. Rain is on the way.

The woods are much thinner than last week, but they aren't bare yet. A grove of tulip trees wears yellow crowns that tower over the woods and glow when the sun breaks through. Suddenly, a gust sends a golden wave of leaves down the hill and over me. It seems like the trees have shaken loose from summer in one glittering moment solely for my ecstasy. I am overwhelmed. Leaves pour over me, rattling as they ricochet from branch to branch in a swirl of yellow. Were they to tinkle as they fall, like coins, I would only smile. There is no finer mint. And when they are at last all scattered at my feet, I look back up the hill and find the trees have only tithed for me; they still glow when the sun breaks through.

But now the clouds thicken. The wind is strengthening. As I'm dressed for rain, I continue on a path that diverges from the loop, up the hill through a grove of mature oaks to a little opening in the secondary growth at the top. I stand at its edge, waiting, as is my wont, for what may happen. A scent of death wafts by. Many things fly on the wind. The sky grows dark. The rattle of dry unfallen leaves becomes almost metallic. The rain's first drops tap at them. Suddenly a young buck is in the clearing. He walks quietly into the trees about twenty yards from me and shakes off the rain with a smooth muscular undulation. He scratches behind his ear with his hind foot, then moves on. His silent path leads behind me and downwind. Many things fly on the wind, and suddenly, I am one of them. He lifts his head straight up, sniffs, snorts, and looks anxiously my way. I am a statue. And, being young, he leaves it at that. Without another sound, he slouches slowly away to disappear at last into the hawthorns.

October 30

The temperature is in the low fifties. High cirrus clouds are drifting in. It's a mild, pleasant day, but we've had hard frosts and a little snow this week, and I am impressed by what is missing.

The clusters of poison ivy berries that nearly covered the old willow by the pond are gone! A rosebush at the tree's base still has most of its rose hips. In fact, there are rose hips, bittersweet, and the blue viburnum berries in abundance.

Poison ivy berries must be a delicacy. I don't see the yellow-rumped warblers today, either. I wonder if they've left, now that we're out of the good stuff.

With its leaves gone, the nearby sassafras tree that was covered with bittersweet has emerged as two trees. Both fork at about mid-height, which makes them look

like Siamese Y's with a red sari draped across their breasts and over a shoulder.

The apple tree by the pond is bare, except for a handful of bronzed and mottled apples—centenarians that haven't seen fit to fall in with the cycle yet. In the woods, the tulip trees have given their all: their gold lies at their feet. The beeches and locust still cling to a few mementos of summer, and the oaks have full crowns, though they're crinkling and brown. As I sit under one of them, the only sounds—after the chipmunks have become bored with me—are the rustling of oak leaves above and gentle taps as some of them flutter down to begin the process anew.

One lone hornet crawls among the leaves. Swarms of delicate little midges dance in beams of sunlight. But, even at noon, there are no butterflies in the meadow or dragonflies on the pond.

Last week's "shriekers" seem to be gone, too. I had supposed that they were bullfrogs in the grass beside the pond. I've heard (and seen) bullfrogs shriek as they dive for deeper water, and tadpoles in the pond look like bullfrog tadpoles. Anyway, they were lively last week, but seem to have gone to bottom now.

But it's too easy, with November pressing close upon us, to dwell on the missing. Life goes on, and joyously. White-throated sparrows scamper under the bushes by the outlet stream. One is eating rose-hips and singing loudly in the marsh. Not to be outdone, a Carolina wren tootles from a treetop. Song sparrows are eating white snakeroot seeds by the pond. A red-tailed hawk with a big notch at the juncture of the secondary and primary feathers on its left wing circles above. A mixed flock of small birds: jays, chickadees, titmice, cardinals, and downy and red-bellied woodpeckers, noisily sweeps along the Braille Trail stream. I think, when I wax nostalgic, I wax for myself alone.

November

Goose Summer Canoeing

Time floats; a leaf
upon a lazy current
may be going somewhere—
maybe not. It pirouettes serenely
on the little whirlwinds
my languid paddle leaves behind,
trails astern sedately,
a milepost for those going nowhere.

Water fleas skip lightly
on the water, leaving
fleeting circles in their wakes.
My little cyclones, too, dissolve:
below, the daphnia forget
the hurricane that spun
their sunlit dance—and so dance on.
Seeds upon the water, spider babies rest:
they'd cast themselves upon a breeze,
sailed upon their gossamer to me,
moored their threads upon my hat, `
and now, their diaspora done,
rest upon a sparkling film
too delicate for human feet.

But November warmth is fragile.
A ghost of chilly premonition
stirs the mirror under me,
whispers of a setting sun, `
foretells an ice-age for the daphnia.
My paddle moves more quickly,
the cyclones swirl behind,
and now I'm making time.

November 6

On a cold, clear morning, the moon hangs low in a blue sky above the gold of the remaining maple leaves at the pond's west end. A rim of ice lies on the pond. The mud crunches. Juncos and white-throated sparrows scratch in the leaves at the base of a large willow. Nearby, goldfinches sway on the tan crowns of goldenrod. Two nuthatches scramble all over the willow tree, upside down.

The tree's core is exposed where a large branch broke off, and one nuthatch is digging into it much as a woodpecker might. Wood chips fly as he digs. I hadn't noticed how sturdy their beaks are until today, and had never heard that they can go at a tree so aggressively.

Nuthatches can be pretty vocal, and this pair has been talking back and forth in their raspy little voices. Even with their talk, I've been struck by the quietness of the morning. But a kingfisher rattles through, and is quickly followed by a red-bellied woodpecker that stays to hammer at a tree. Several jays come in with bedlam in their wake. I can't tell what they're carrying on about.

It seems like a good time to explore the hillside south of the Braille Trail's little stream. Last week, I'd gone north. This hill is pretty steep and is home to a grove of huge old oaks, hickories, and beeches. Rather distressingly, masses of grape vines hang from and swarm over many of the trees. Some of the trees seem to be dead or dying. I wonder whether this is a new and spreading phenomenon caused, perhaps, by fragmentation of the forests, or if it's a competition as old as the last glaciation.

"Fragmentation" refers to breaks in forests due to roads, developments, clear-cuts, etc. Natural breaks, such as those caused by avalanches and fires, seem to be important food sources for the forest wildlife. But they're isolated and temporary. Permanent inroads invite invasion of shade-loving species by the sun-loving. For example, cowbirds evolved as followers of the bison on the prairies. As the bison moved, so did they, and so developed the practice of laying their eggs in other birds' nests. Many prairie birds learned, in time, to identify and destroy cowbird eggs. Cowbirds won't venture far into a forest, but as fragmentation has opened more forest edges to them, their parasitism has become a major problem for ground-nesting deep-forest warblers that haven't evolved a defense.

Every crow in the county seems to be congregated at the top of the hill, and every one has a lot to say. I'm reminded of the ranting of politicians on talk shows, but it's surely an avian, not a human mobbing. A large owl probably sits unhappily in the middle of it. There's a lot of clicking midst the cawing. I haven't heard that before and wonder if that's the owl, talking back. But I can't find an owl. Since there are a couple of bow hunters' stands in the trees nearby, maybe the attraction is the offal from a kill. But I can't find that, either. At last the crows straggle off to the west and I am left with another mystery. TV shows and movies usually end with the package neatly tied, but I often leave the woods with unused paper and string, and a lot of unwrapped little episodes.

November 12

After a wild night of wind and rain, a gray but quiet sky hangs heavily over the Braille Trail in late afternoon. The little stream is full, but not boisterous. Tall wine-stained pokeweeds, bedraggled and broken, lean across a deer trail on the northern hillside. Their berries are nearly gone. The barberry bushes have lost their leaves, but not their berries. Perhaps that's because they're aliens and less favored by the local wildlife; maybe it's because there are just lots more of them. In any case, the berries gleam in the twilight like bright red lanterns. Shelf-mushrooms gnawing on a dead elm are clothed in more somber brown and dark yellow. *(I think they're called mustard-yellow polypores.)* Bright green Christmas ferns are scattered across the hillside.

Such are the musings of a birdwatcher when the woods are very quiet. But birdwatchers are a jumpy sort: we learn to look for small movements at the edges of our eyes. That works well in springtime, not so well in autumn. For the umpteenth time, I jerk to attention to focus on a small leaf's last flutter and slow tumble into some other tree's tomorrow.

One of those quick glances just landed on a bit of woodland magic I still can't unravel: the leap of a grapevine into the top of a tall tree. Beside me, an inch-thick vine hangs straight down from the top of a young beech tree. From there, it has jumped a ten foot gap into the branches of an old oak, which it then snakes to the top of. Indeed, it looks like a seventy foot python draped in the trees. Cold yellow eyes would explain the grapevines' gymnastics. Yes, I rather like that answer. But hanging from another oak nearby are a dozen thinner vines, rather like pirates' boarding lines flung into the rigging of a doomed schooner. Lots of thin lines flung upward, and then consolidation—that sounds more likely—but I still like the snake eyes theory.

Another bit of amazement: even on cold days, fragile-looking insects float by on gossamer wings. Why aren't they frozen into cold-blooded rigidity, insect-statues tucked away on hidden pedestals? But one just sailed by on urgent business of its own, though the temperature is only 40°.

At last, a fluttering among the branches really is a bird! Several, in fact. A little troop of chickadees and titmice appear in the oaks and tulip trees up the hill and to the left of me. Quietly and methodically, they frisk each tree and move on. Somewhere nearby, a woodpecker knocks softly. Titmice, chickadees, downy woodpeckers—such flocks usually hold other species as well. But all I see today are tiny silhouettes flitting among stark black branches against a gray background. Except one. As the main flock disappears over the shoulder of the hill to my right, a small brown bird appears, climbing straight up the smooth lichen-patched bark of a young white oak. It's a brown creeper! It isn't a rare bird, according to the manuals, but most of us don't see many of them. In typical creeper fashion, it walks up the tree, pecking at insects along the way, then flies to the base of the next tree on the flock's path, hunts up the trunk of that one, and so it trails along behind the others.

As evening falls around me, I walk the Braille Trail home. And here I find another bit of magic: springtime in November! The witch hazels are in bloom! Some of the spidery yellowish flowers are nearly hidden among mottled brown and yellow leaves that haven't yet given up the year, but most wriggle out of branches that are otherwise quite naked.

Perhaps this was the business that drew that determined little bug out on a cold November day.

November 20

This morning, the brown goldenrod heads are sugared with frost. Leaves of hickory and oak, crisp with morning ice, lay scattered across the woodland floor. Their edges and veins, traced in white, might grace a child's coloring book. Indeed, the whole woods is traced by a thin pencil in brown and white: stark, brittle with cold, yet lovely. My breath floats ahead of me as I crunch up the hill above the Braille Trail.

At the top of the hill, as I rest against a huge old oak, the sun begins to trace its bright arc in the southern sky and the last echoes of my footsteps march into the valley below. A red squirrel appears high in a sibling of my oak, at the very fringe where tree and blue sky merge. It's 80 feet above the frozen floor—at least. One hundred, maybe. But to the squirrel, the tree is a superhighway in Iowa: flat and broad, with no traffic. It races nonchalantly down its vertical path, unconcerned with height. "Earth" is just a left turn. At the tree's base, it patters across the leaves without a thought. "Horizontal" and "vertical" have no meaning for squirrels; to them, the world is flat.

To me, though, the world of the treetops is a mystery, traveled only in imagination. Better that I try to walk the pond's skim ice than to attempt to retrace that squirrel's brief stroll. Two robins land among the same thin boughs, gaze about from the top of everything, scold something they alone can see, and leave. They dwell just as easily in that impossible world. I, though, am standing earthbound below, craning my neck like a tourist in New York City.

Still, even from the ground, winter's spare brush unveils much of the structure summer hides. The massive oak flows like a river of wood from capillary rivulets in the sun down tributary branches to the great brown flood and thence into the sea of earth. Stripped of its green curtains, the valley lays like a map below. Rills fall into the stream, deer paths find the easiest lines across and down the hill, small nests, so well hidden in June, spring out as round cups among vertical lines.

It was in this time of nakedness that Loren Eiseley found himself, as he grew older, searching for the secret of life, examining "in sharp and beautiful angularity the shape of life without its disturbing muddle of juices and leaves". Natural enough for a "bone-man", a paleontologist with a poetic twist. Most of us have dismantled a dead radio to learn what made it run. And most of us have learned, from a loose connection or a bare wire, that the secret is electric. But what is unplugged when a heart stops? What is lost so suddenly that we can speak of "the moment of death"? Or, more to the point, what are we plugged into?

Eiseley wrote in the days just before Watson and Crick found the shape of DNA, but I think that, had he been privy to today's biochemistry, he would still have found his search incomplete. Then, he sought the secret in the geometries of death. Today, we tend to peer right into that muddle of juices to seek the secret among the arrows and arcane symbols of chemistry. But what is lost when, as Eiseley says, "at the instant of death…that ordered, incredible spinning passes away in an almost furious haste of those same particles to get themselves back into the chaotic, unplanned earth"? He came to doubt—as have I—that the question can be answered. We sense that something lies far deeper than the skulls of mice and DNA, something indefinable that finds expression in the soft plunge of owl on mouse and the drumming heartbeat of a migrant in the night. I believe, more and more, that I'll find my way in wonder, for I cannot understand.

Wonder brought me here to seek, as deeply as I can, expressions of the Great Unknowable among the trees and waters of this tiny wilderness.

And as I muse, leaves fall about me in twos and threes. Oak leaves have collected, or were gathered, in the broken top of a cherry tree that stands nearby. There, a Carolina wren is rummaging for something, tossing leaves right and left like a kid going through a drawer for a matched pair of socks. At last it finds what it's looking for and drops like a rock, with a prize in its bill, into a hole at my feet. The "hole" is a little opening in a tangle of brush, grapevines, and leaves. I suspect that there is a warm space inside, for steam rises from it in the early sunshine. Carolina wrens are, or were, at the northern boundaries they can survive. That tangle may be the solution for at least one of them.

A flock of nuthatches, titmice, and chickadees is passing through. From the woods east of me, either a flicker or a pileated woodpecker calls. I'm unsure which.

Suddenly, I am sure. A female (*no red below the eye line?*) pileated flies through like a black spear, to land just below a large dead limb in the big oak.

She taps tentatively, working both up and down the tree. She finds the spot, finally, and bark and wood fall in chunks. She chisels away for awhile, then pokes and pecks at whatever she's uncovered. More chiseling, more tidbits, and so the morning goes. She digs so deeply that, after a while, her whole head fits into the hole. She works so hard that I wonder if she's putting more energy into the tree than she's getting. The picture is dramatic: a jet-black silhouette against the tree that flashes red and white in the sunlight as she hammers. A titmouse lands on a branch just below, and watches her. It seems to be waiting for tidbits to fall, or her to leave before they're all gone. Neither happens, so the titmouse leaves. And two red squirrels chasing up the tree freeze just below her. One runs back down, the other stays, flattened on the trunk a foot or two below her. This seems to be a challenge. The woodpecker leaps to the branch above, spreads her wings, and suddenly she's a huge black pterodactyl, glaring down her stiletto and hissing! I blink; the squirrel runs back down the tree.

She goes back to her work.

Finally, and without warning, she drops from the tree and silently floats through the woods like a sharp black shadow. I've been wondering if the hole is rectangular, like the ones left by pileated woodpeckers by Walter Road. It isn't. It's nearly perfectly round. Wood chips the size of a fingernail lay among the leaves at the base of the tree. I expected that. I didn't expect the big mushy chunks of bracket fungus. She must have been digging behind that.

Down the hill, now, to the Braille Trail and its stream. I've wanted to collect some witch hazel seedpods. The view from the south-facing hillside is lovely. Two kinds of fern--Christmas fern and spinulose woodfern (?)--are glistening green against the tan of oak and tulip leaves. The witch hazels are feathery yellow in the sunlight. The scene could be from April, except for the tattered leaves impaled on and lodged in the naked fingers of the other trees.

I do pick a few seedpods. They're soft, wet, and about the size of the tip of my little finger. Later, I put them on a high—cat-free—shelf to dry, thinking that I'll have a few days to find a jar before they explode. During the afternoon of the next day, I hear a loud pop. They haven't waited for me. That was the last one, and I can't find any seeds. Witch hazel will probably be sprouting from my rug next spring.

December

If I had known

While walking the Company's road,
my tight, sleet-driven steps crunched to a stop
before a nest I'd missed in May.
It was a solid nest, of twigs and mud

and shreds of confidential documents
(appropriated from our trash bin)
swaying stiffly in the wind,
like frozen laces on an outgrown baby shoe.

December's icy hands had stripped it,
wrapped themselves around the cup of snow
to tend the remnants of a mother's work,
to gather up the castoffs from her dream.

But in warmer winds, she'd wrapped her secrets
in those scraps of ours and mothered furtively.
We worker bees, entranced by busyness, buzzed
unaware beneath her patient sitting.

We missed the metamorphosis
from silent, turquoise eggs
to gaping, squawking mouths
with sightless eyes and naked wings.

We missed her tireless, cautious hunts
to still those boisterous beaks,
to fill those wings with sky, one day,
and leave that sacred place irrelevant.

We missed all that. I wish I'd known.
But not to peer into another's mystery.
For countless shattered nests
in Mays gone by have taught me

of the hungry eyes of jays and cats,
of perils lurking in the loveliest days.
No, I would have walked by gently
and, smiling, looked the other way.

December 5

Days like this make global warming seem very real. At 10:00, the sun is shining in a cloudless sky and the temperature is already in the low sixties. By midday, it's likely that this will have been the hottest December 5 in history.

Astronomically, though, it really is December. And when the sun hangs just above a wooded hill in winter, its light angling low glistens on bare twigs and cobwebs in concentric circles, as though the trees were cupping their branches around the sun for warmth. I haven't noticed the effect in summer. Perhaps it's one of those symmetries that only nakedness reveals.

I wonder if most of us really know what to do with such a day. In May, the woods would be alive with breeding and rearing; in October, they would be busy with fattening up and flying away. But all that's done, so what to do now? I suspect that many are just napping. A large doe, annoyed that I would stare as she dozes, snorts and walks off over the hill. She doesn't seem to have the energy to raise her flag.

Deer often cross paths with me in North Park. Sometimes, they see me first. Often though, if I'm standing very still and the wind isn't blowing from me to them, they seem unable to tell what, exactly, I am. Not quite alarmed, curious but wary, they glare at me (with their ears, too, if that's possible), stamp their feet, and make a sound like an exasperated, wheezy sneeze. I've used "snort", "huff", and "whuff" to describe it. As a writer, I prefer not to overuse such words, but these encounters are common. So you'll hear a lot of snorting.

A flock of small birds is reasonably active. A chickadee hangs upside down from a shred of caterpillar tent and shreds it further. A pair of titmice pokes about in the cracks and crevices of a dead elm. A downy woodpecker knocks hollowly on its trunk to see, perhaps, if the bark beetles are at home. A jay bathes in the stream amidst flying jewels of spray. Crows converse languidly in the distance. As the sun moves west along the ridge, riffles in the stream sparkle hypnotically. The air and my eyes grow heavier...

December 11

Winter is back. It's a cold, clear day. Frost frames the last stiff leaves of the multiflora rose and powders its red berries. The northwest corner of the pond is covered by skim ice. The rest of the pond, though, is a still, liquid mirror. Half of the mirror lies in shadow, half in sunshine. A forest grows within the mirror, upside down, but sharp and clear. The trees are stark and somber in the depths that lie in shadow. A crow flies just below the surface, a tiny black spider-shape rowing across the gray sky, portending, perhaps, some bleak tomorrow? Not at all, for on the sunny side, the sky below is blue. There the trees, while bare as their dark brethren, glow in the light, more even than their air-breathing twins. And everywhere, as little fish nip holes in the sky, the trees waver and dance on the ripples.

A young red-shouldered hawk floats in, lands on a dead branch in a flare of white wings, preens and fluffs herself, then settles to let the pond forget her. She leans forward and peers up at me. Up? No, down. She is very real, and shakes me from my reverie. But I'm too big to eat and too still to quite make out. Her cold yellow gaze sweeps past me and up the shore.

"We are similar, you and I," I mutter. "I arrived more humbly, surely, but just as obviously, leaned against this tree, stuck my hands in my pockets, and waited for stillness to turn me into a stump. And I do hunt, in my way. The difference is that I have eaten."

That is no small difference. She sees nothing edible, launches on heavy wings, and disappears over the northern hills. I doubt that she was looking at reflections. Or reflecting. A grumbling belly is so very practical.

The morning grows louder as it awakes. Crows are mobbing something in the hills—the hawk, perhaps. Several very large and very loud flocks of geese fly west in V's. The usual flock of resident birds passes through. In the distance, someone hammers incessantly.

The crows are louder, I suppose, and I own a hammer, too, but this intrusion from the borders of my wilderness seems louder than its decibels. And the morning chill has seeped inside my jacket. So the carpenter and the cold send me exploring. I tuck my binoculars under my arm and launch myself up the hills to follow the hawk.

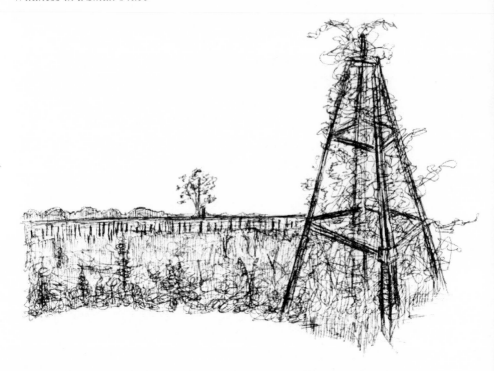

The upper meadow: windmill tower and sycamore tree

Up the hill north of the pond on the boy scout trail, beyond some early-growth woodland, I find a jewel! On the map, it's called the "upper field". It appears to be just that, a large (*thirty acres, I learned later*) fallow field surrounded by woods. And it bristles with birdhouses. Perched on the houses and an abundance of mullein are bluebirds. A whole flock! I stand quietly under an old windmill tower that is blanketed by bittersweet, and watch. Flocks of robins, several field sparrows and cardinals, and one mockingbird pass through. I will watch this field as the year flows toward spring.

Common mullein is a biannual alien in the snapdragon family. Initially, it's a low rosette of large velvety leaves, but during its second year it sends up a spire of small yellow flowers that can be six feet tall. It makes a wonderful lookout for birds and, apparently, is a good source of food. Gibb Merrill, a naturalist at Elmira College, said that, in winter, mullein is a "bug hotel".

December 17

More than half of the pond gleams the dull white of snowy ice beneath the barren gray of a late dawn. Though this isn't the shortest day, it very nearly is. The chill probes my jacket at the neckline and sleeves. The daytime sounds froze and fell to earth overnight. Some are just beginning to thaw: the rush of water down the outlet stream, calls of distant crows, urgent twitters of goldfinches. But mostly, the woods echo only the crunching of my boots on brittle snow.

Walking is warmer, but I see more standing still, so I take a post by a large oak on the hill that overlooks the Braille Trail. Icy stillness reigns for long minutes. My nose drips. My skin feels tight. A Carolina wren chirrs in the trees higher up the hill. Now the soft tap, tap, tap of a downy woodpecker floats up from the trees beside the pond. And again, silence.

Christmas ferns lie in the snow beside the deer path. They're still intact—their leaves look like little green boots strung on a line—but they seem rather trampled. Perhaps that's the deer's doing, or maybe it's just the effect of the cold.

51

Farther up the hill, nuts lie in a pile at the base of a large oak. The black walnuts are gnawed and hollow, but some of the hickory nuts seem intact. Oddly, there are no acorns in the collection. And no squirrel in sight.

Nearby, a large hollow log stretches across the hillside, its slow journey back into the earth in winter hiatus. It's nearly bone-bare; one small patch of bark remains, gray-green with moss. The patch looks a bit like eczema. Snow encrusts the length of the log like a little Chinese wall running along the crest of a mountain. The snow has left the brown oak leaves that lie in swathes around it, but the log retains this remnant. On the hillside, white gleams only from the angles of living limbs and from this log. Though it must be earth again, it will not yet give up this last memory of its treeness.

Beyond the log, a gray squirrel crosses the leaves in long leaps. Across the valley, the pileated woodpecker rattles, then knocks loudly. A troop of small birds—chickadees, titmice, nuthatches—pass over, chattering to each other. Cardinals land as a flock in the bittersweet. For long loud minutes, the trees' bare fingers reach out to hold the living. But at last the troop rattles over the top of the hill and I march down to the stream.

Deer must have trampled those ferns up the hill. By the stream, both the Christmas ferns and the woodferns are still green and healthy-looking. *(Spinulose woodferns are lacy "thrice-cut" ferns that look very much like those we buy in florist shops.)* The witch hazel blossoms, on the other hand, are shriveled and brown. And spring seems very far away.

December 30

But now the days grow longer. Imperceptibly longer, yes, but longer. This morning dawned, at last, red in a cold clear sky. Rain is expected in the afternoon, but now, snow covers the ground and lies heavily on the branches. In a corner of the "upper meadow," a thicket of brambles bows beneath its weight. The wild tangle of hooks that would shred me if I cared to challenge it has been humbled by—just snow. And the wild Macedonian spears were tamed into the phalanx by—just Alexander!

This particular thicket of spears seems to lie upon a woodland crossroads. Deer paths funnel from the meadow into the woods here. Invisible paths above my head have brought cardinals, jays, titmice, and chickadees, and more pass as I write. A sparrow of some sort flutters among the brambles as it nibbles rose hips, viburnum berries, and bittersweet, leaving little snowfalls behind as it leaves one to find another. Above, two crows labor over silently. Tracks of a large dog and many rabbits crisscross about my feet. There is a tale in those tracks. It likely ends with a tired but happy hound panting at the edge of the brambles and one, or several, rabbits peering out, unscathed, from behind the curtain of thorns.

To paraphrase an old punch line, with so many pellets lying around, there must be a bunny in here somewhere. But not obviously. In my younger days, we solved such puzzles with the "stomp around and shoot when they run" technique. My uncle was more sophisticated. As a boy, he had helped feed his family with rabbits and squirrels during the Depression, and had learned to see them before they ran and shoot them with a slingshot. He said the trick was to look for their eyes. I'm looking for round black eyes among the brambles, but am seeing only brambles. Perhaps rabbits weren't so well camouflaged during the Depression. Perhaps, today, their eyes are closed in slumber. Perhaps. Or maybe those who must hunt or starve look more closely and see more clearly than the rest of us.

The claws of the multiflora rose aren't to be trifled with in any case but, last summer, those of one bush in the meadow must have been the envy of the hosts of the hooked and barbed. The bush itself is chest-high, which isn't unusual. But among its lower branches, at about knee-height, bald-faced hornets built a nest the size of a basketball. Tolkien missed a throw when he left this nastiness out of Mordor. During the summer, it was a buzzing ball of evil-tempered darts built on and surrounded by the barbed wire bush—and at a height where the unwary might come to grief. The hornets have left it now, and snow lies on its forehead. It's a tattered visage, with strips of paper hanging from its chin. But it still looks mean. Hooked stems protrude from the top like devilish horns.

I'm told that the hanging paper is often a sign that field mice have built their own winter nest inside, and that foxes are aware of this. Woe to the fox that tries to tear this nest apart!

Nearby, in a second bush much like the first, snow fills a small round nest tucked neatly among the thorns. The nest seems to be woven from the meadow grasses, which suggests a red-winged blackbird. For some reason, I approve of those little daggers when they're defending small birds. But protecting hornets seems to break some rule of sensibility.

As I cross the meadow, a male cardinal races overhead with a mockingbird in close pursuit. December is an odd time to be territorial.

On the other side of the meadow, the woods sound like a dripping faucet. The snow is leaving in droplets, puffs of white, and a fine mist that fogs my binoculars. Trees are glistening ebony columns looming in the mist. This could be the original "Arrangement in Black and Gray". Could be, except for several bluebirds flitting in and out of a bush of red berries. Bluebirds' blue is so vivid—I think they could make even the hornets' bush lovely.

January

Balance

If spring is a splash of pastel
on a bright green wash
in exuberant strokes
by the rowdy committee
of wide-eyed chattering young
who just can't wait to grow
up,

then winter is drawn
on a cold white sheet
in thin black lines
by the Clerk's tight hand,
frugal and precise,
leaving all that's unessential
out.

January 9

Over the weekend, several inches of snow fell and temperatures were in the twenties. Today, the temperature is about 40°, so the snow is melting. But the sky is gray, the sun a diffuse blob of light hanging just above the southern ridge at Latodami, and the wind is rising as the afternoon wanes. Ice and snow cover the pond, though the outlet area and the stream are clear. There, melting snow from overhanging limbs plinks into perfect rings. In early December, those ripples could run the breadth of the pond and wrinkle the faces of trees. Now, they run only to the ice-edges of a very narrow mirror. Perhaps they run on beneath the ice for those with dreams of summer.

Chickadees and cardinals forage among the branches, jays fly over and by on sentry duty, and crows mob something in the distance. The rose hips are nearly gone from the pond area.

In the "upper meadow," there are deer tracks all around, but no deer to be seen. The rose hips are nearly gone there, too, but there is a lot of bittersweet still. Field and song sparrows hunt at the edge of the meadow. I'd love to see an owl, so I stalk through a stand of pine and spruce at the meadow's western edge, peering up the conifer boles. Perhaps great round eyes gaze back down at me from the dark recesses above. If so, they must blink lazily at a creature too blind to fear, to big to eat. The woodpeckers have been active: white lines of congealed sap run down the pine trunks from neat round holes farther up. A Carolina wren pokes about in the bushes, and a small black and white bird hunts the bark of black locust from base to boughs. It looks and acts just like a brown creeper, but it's the wrong color! Whatever else it may be, it certainly is patient with me. I trail behind, binoculars aimed directly at it, as it hunts through a dozen trees. My best guess is that it's a gray-phase brown creeper. Perhaps it's accustomed to celebrity.

January 14

The breeding and nesting time for hawks and owls approaches. Theirs is one of the first cogs that slips into place as the year's wheel turns: their chicks must hatch just when prey becomes abundant. Incubation takes about a month and, of course, there is the mating and nesting before, so if they are to catch the first rodent litters and the early migrants and nesters, they must start early. I've noticed a large snow-filled nest among the trees on the hillside across the road from the barn, and today seems like a good day to check on it.

So, on another cold gray day, I hike up that hill. Though the sun has had nearly a whole day to warm the world, it has failed even to show up. The temperature is sliding. Snow floats down in soft diaphanous flakes. This is "lake effect snow," the scientific term for Lake Erie, migrating inland.

Trails, both of deer and humans, lead upward. I choose a deer's path. It meanders upward through bushes and saplings—I've been told that this hillside was a pasture not many years ago. Rabbit tracks wander among the bushes; rabbit pellets are scattered about and lie, especially, in little clumps at the bases of the bushes. One species of bush—I can't identify it without its leaves—seems to be both preferred dining room and toilet. Just above the piles of little round pellets, the bark has been gnawed and stripped. And I am humbled by this abundance of rabbit sign: though I'm surrounded by footprints, I haven't seen a foot.

Higher up the hill, I find several nests scattered among the tops of young trees. They aren't hawks' nests: they're too small, too flimsy, and too many. Hawks don't nest in clusters. These nests are flat, rather loose accumulations of twigs. They're reminiscent of mourning dove nests, but bigger. I don't know whose they were.

At the top of the hill lies the "lower meadow". In November, I watched the pileated woodpecker from its western border, but this is the first time I've approached it from the north. Earlier, I'd seen a large nest on the southern edge, so I stand just inside the tree line to look for signs that it's in use.

The north wind has risen a bit; the snowfall is heavier. I'm growing ever whiter as I lean against a large black cherry tree, wondering where the hawks might be, when an owl looms over me. It was flying along the tree line about ten feet above the ground and went right over me to land in another tree nearby. I could have touched it with my walking stick. But I was too preoccupied with owlishness in daylight to identify it. Now I see only its back as it peers through the snow into the meadow. It swoops to the ground, leans down, looks back up and all around, then returns to its perch. After many minutes, it moves farther to my right to another perch. I do want to know what it is, so I follow, certain that I'll scare it away, but willing to risk it. I do get closer, its back is still facing me, and it doesn't spook. It swoops into the meadow again, and I see a brown, maybe streaked breast, no "ears". It returns to its perch, mostly obscured by intervening trees. Suddenly, soundlessly, it's right above me once again. It floats down the line of trees to a new perch; I catch my breath. I had hoped it would come back. I was waiting for it. But when it did, I froze. The world was suddenly brown and white, with big brown eyes. If, when it fills the air above them, the mice are as petrified as I, this owl eats well.

I do know its name though. It's a barred owl, a species of owl that will hunt in half light. It seems not to care if I watch, so I do. Always with its back to the wind, it perches and swoops two or three more times, farther and farther down the tree line and then among the oaks at the east end of the meadow. My last vision of the owl is in the binoculars' circle: a brown figure, leaning forward slightly from its perch among bare brown branches, with snow streaming between us to dapple and obscure.

(I had thought that, since it didn't spend much time on the ground, the owl wasn't catching anything. Sibley says, though, that owls often swallow their prey whole, and spend little time on the ground. That fits what I saw.)

Strix varia

January 18

I'm hunting owls again. I missed a rare opportunity last time so, today, I'm going to try to make up for it. The prints that hawks and owls make when they stoop upon prey in the snow are supposed to be dramatic. But I was so busy watching the owl that I forgot to look for the prints. Today, I'll see if the owl will grant me a repeat performance.

As before, I'm standing among the trees that line the north side of the lower meadow. Alas, this time, I forgot my binoculars! I feel naked without them. I'd almost rather that I'd forgotten my pants.

Well, maybe not. The temperature is 15° and falling, in spite of occasional visits by the low, late afternoon sun. The chill is much lower: a cold wind flows across my eyeballs. There seem to be ice cubes in my sinuses.

Wrapping my muffler around my face helps a lot. I'm pretty comfortable now, but the vigil seems futile. A junco sat in a nearby bush for a while, and a large woodpecker flew over. It was probably a red-bellied woodpecker, but without binoculars, I couldn't be sure. There is no owl, either.

There may be more activity at the "bird and animal crossroad" at the northeast corner of the upper meadow. There are more berries there, anyway, and the hike will warm me.

As I arrive at the upper meadow, a little flock of cedar waxwings flush from the bushes, fly a tight circle into the meadow and back into the top of a nearby tree to watch me for a while. Soon, they drop back into the multiflora rose to resume their meal. Ten or fifteen minutes later, they fly off into the woods. I'm standing alone, surrounded by empty trees above, rabbit tracks and rabbit pellets in the snow below.

Two observations occur to me. First, the birds I've seen, the waxwings and the junco, are at the southern edge of their ranges. Even they seem to be conserving energy. The rest of the avian population—and mammal, too—seem to be curled up in the warmest places they know. Second, although I'm out in the cold, I'm also wearing most of the winter clothing I own. But all of these other creatures own only themselves: their feathers or fur, the layer of fat they've been able to accumulate, their genetic wisdom, and whatever they've learned in their short lives. As the sun fell into an autumn evening, many of Latodami's summer inhabitants packed themselves up, leaped into the night sky, and vanished into the darkness on odysseys that few human adventures could match. Whole species do that, twice a year, to avoid nights like tonight. Those who stayed will spend the night huddled over their inner fires, waiting for the dawn. The next few dawns will offer only a cold light.

Another observation: the absence of the meadow's larger inhabitants leaves space for meditation upon the small. Often, when the world is snow, I look for springtails. These tiny primitive insects with switchblade tails are inhabitants of leaf duff, usually. I think that only an entomologist could find them there. But sometimes they gather to bounce upon the snow like a pinch of pepper on a tightly-made bed. I don't know why. Perhaps this ballet of Olympian leaps from spring-loaded tails is their version of the airy mating dances of the midges. I also don't know if, when they wish, they can walk in the regular way or if, for them, every step is a leap into the unknown—dots doomed to travel in dashes. I wonder how our lives would be if every step whisked us a hundred yards away.

None appear today, but the midges do. They seem frail—wisps of insects with lace for wings—but they walk the snow and flit through the icy air as though the hot blood of birds pulses through their capillary-thin thoraxes. But they, like the springtails, carry the ancient blood, only a generation removed from the waters of rivers and, like those waters, prone to freeze. So how do they walk the cold earth, and why?

A shiver shakes me back to the frigid, empty field. The sun is sinking even lower among the hills. So, highly evolved and warm-blooded though I may be, prudence says to leave the meadow to the primitives that thrive there. I want a warm place to curl up in.

January 22

It's still cold. Surely the wise are curled up in burrows, wrapped in their tails. But I get cabin fever. So despite the chill, I'm walking the upper meadow to see what I can see.

First are bluebirds sitting on a couple of the birdhouses. A cheerful beginning. And the usual winter birds fly over or forage in the area: crows, jays, robins, starlings, chickadees, titmice, downy woodpeckers, and cardinals. But they don't stay long or do much. The jays and titmice are vocal occasionally, but most of the time, the only sounds are of the wind and my clumsy feet on crusty snow. Dry brown grasses and tatters of goldenrod—no longer at all golden—bow in the breezes.

The wise are moving only as they must, and hoard their heat. I, however, still can't face four walls—and walk on.

I am rewarded! A line of small round prints in the snow traces the meadow's edge. They look like fox tracks. I would dearly love to see a fox. I've seen many through the years. One leaped and pounced for mice in heavy snow. Two kits played at the edge of their den till mom came home, saw me, and sent them flickering down the hole with one sharp bark. And one, on a hot summer day, wandered, rabid and undone, in sad circles of despair. But mostly, they've been like meteors: a flash of fire and gone. Like meteors, I know where to look for them, but they appear if and as they please. Both leave me feeling that something of wonder and mystery has passed.

I think, though, that in the case of the fox at least, that feeling has more to do with "wildness" than with "fox-ness". I can see the shape of a fox any time—in a zoo. Yet the shape of a fox lying panting in the dirt with no place to go and nothing much to do is not—for me—a fox. The essence of a fox, or deer, or any other living thing is, first of all, free will. I know the arguments for zoos, and I don't doubt their truth. Still, I always leave such places sadder. I'd rather see footprints in the snow.

January 29

I've come to the edge of the lower meadow to check on the hawk's nest again. Loitering with the birds today should be unusually comfortable for a January morning. It's warm and likely to get warmer. Rain has been forecast, but so far, the sky is only partially overcast with patches of blue.

I seem to see the most animal life if I just stand quietly by a large tree. After ten or fifteen minutes, I must blend into the background. I've been standing by a huge oak just inside the woods for an hour or so. The usual winter birds have passed through a couple of times: jays, chickadees, titmice, a very vocal red-bellied woodpecker, a pair of nuthatches, song sparrows, a downy woodpecker, and a kinglet. I couldn't tell which kinglet, since it stayed high in the trees with the sun at its back. Occasional checks for activity in the large nest across the meadow have shown none. Neither have I seen a pair of hawks in the area. Perhaps this is too early in the year. Perhaps the nest won't be used at all.

February

A walk in thin times

The snow, in anguish, groans beneath me
as I stalk a land of chandeliers and lace.
It lies thick and heavy on the land,
glistening and barren, but for shadows
sketched skeletal and vague upon it.

It lays heavy, too, upon the spruce—
born of winter, they but shrug
their shoulders, bow a bit, and bear it.

Hickories, the summer trees,
sift it through their bony fingers;
let it lie in heaps beneath them.

And thin above the mists of morn—
the valley's frozen exhalations—
a pale, myopic sun squints
weakly through their naked branches.

The brittle air is thin and sharp.
Thin too, a squirrel beneath the hickory
mines the drifts for buried nuts:
dives into sparkling tunnels, quickly;
pops back up for sentry duty, but doesn't see
the hawk arrive: white flash
of quiet wings, it settles on a branch,
eyes glittering, leans forward,
an arrow taut upon the string.

And so we stand, we three:
starving hawk and starving squirrel and me.
One looks; one sees.
I watch, wondering
that August sun has flowed
from leaf through nut to fur, and if,
upon this pale thin day,
my choice should be
to let it flow to feather?

February 3

The quarry today is the short-eared owl. The date and time are right, but the weather may not be. The barometer is falling and the wind is stiff and westerly. It's cold, and the sun seems far away and irrelevant. Typical winter clouds scud across the sky: they're gray underneath and not very puffy, like biscuits only partially leavened. Evening is a couple of hours away, but the light is dull already.

I know that short-eared owls winter in the area. A few years ago, a friend and I visited an overgrown strip mine southwest of Pittsburgh with the same goal. As we walked through that meadow, owls flushed ahead of us like pheasants. Dusk was near, so they didn't just settle into the long grass ahead of us. I guess they figured that as long as they were up, they might as well begin the evening hunt. Soon, a couple of dozen were soaring low above the meadow. It must have been a bad day for the mice.

The upper meadow looks a lot like that other field. Perhaps there are owls here, too.

As I approach the meadow, a flicker flushes ahead of me. That seems like a good start. At first, I sit under the old windmill tower, since that gives a good view of the meadow. It's also very open and windswept. A mockingbird flies from its perch in the long hedge that bisects the field to the more protected woods at the meadow's southern edge. Sometimes, I recognize wisdom when I see it. I follow the bird.

Inside the woods, a bluebird flashes bright blue against the drab brown of tattered grasses and naked trees. He is hunting more methodically than I. He sits on a branch that leans out over the meadow's edge, peering into the grasses below. Periodically, he drops into the grass, captures something, and flutters back to his perch with the prize. It's a style much like that of the flycatchers', though not so dramatic—flycatchers swoop from the perch to catch insects as they fly. It's also a style that surprises me at this time of year. He seems to be catching bugs and, though I've seen the midges on the snow, the notion that insects are active when it's so cold still is strange to me. The bluebird isn't limited by such prejudices. And he, not I, can live off the land in winter.

Chickadees are prowling through the branches behind me and the mockingbird is eating bittersweet above my head. That doesn't surprise me. Birds are supposed to eat berries in winter, and I've always assumed that the chickadees were finding dormant bugs and larvae in the cracks and crevices of trees. But who knows? Maybe they're also finding inchworms humping merrily across the icy twigs on a hundred little crampons. I'm learning a lot about my assumptions.

The sun is slipping slowly and horizontally toward the west. Robins scold something in the distance. Finally, as the sun drops below the hills, I hike out and across the meadow. Perhaps the owls will flush ahead of me. The wind rumbles through my hearing aids, the brown grasses bow and wave eastward, and the last few biscuit-ships sail a nearly empty sky.

No owls. Oh well.

February 9

I've no particular goal today. The morning is bright and crisp with high, thin cirrus clouds in a blue sky. The wind is only a whisper today. The pond is frozen, and I doubt that one could glean a hatful of rose hips around it anymore. A chickadee chitters to itself as it hunts among the cattails. Finished with that, it perches on the top of the cinnamon-brown candle of a battered and bent cattail, looks about, and launches toward the woods in the scalloped flight of little birds.

My hike to the hilltop is so noisy that I feel naked. The hillside is littered with frozen leaves that the deer step silently under. (*Years ago, in Michigan, a twelve-point buck was locally famous for his wiliness. On a day just like this he slipped silently through the woods just beyond the range of my bow. Later, I couldn't find his footprints till I looked beneath the leaves. He had walked under them!*) I doubt that I could do that in moccasins; in size 10 1/2 hiking boots I might as well be carrying cymbals. I crunch, I crash, I blush.

At last, with relief, I station myself at the edge of the lower meadow under a big old tulip tree. A titmouse on his rounds among the treetops didn't mind my noise; he's making more. Already, he has whistled more calls than I—or the Audubon tape—realize he knows. So little, yet so versatile and loud! A red squirrel has been watching me from a tree limb, apparently deciding whether or not to announce me to the world. He decides to save his breath; I've announced myself pretty well.

Fifty yards away, a red-bellied woodpecker discretely knocks on a tree. It stays in one tree so long, and works so quietly, that I wonder if it's starting a nest hole. But later when I look at the tree, there is a series of neat round holes up the side. He must have flown away with a very full belly. There are, however, a couple of larger and older nest holes in adjacent trees that will bear watching later.

After the titmouse has finished, the woods are pretty quiet. Occasional crow patrols pass over. A nuthatch rasps in the valley below, a chickadee sings its plaintive mating call, and a flicker (or pileated woodpecker?) rattles from the next hill. A chipmunk sits in the sun on an old log, brushing its whiskers.

By the time I leave, the sun has softened the leaves so I don't crash about so. Still, I feel alone on the hill and long for the first migrants and green upthrusting. But, of course, I'm not alone. A fox squirrel curled in the sun in a high crotch of an oak watches me as I pass by. Eyes I don't see surely watch me, too.

February 23

A turkey vulture flew over a couple of days ago, so the first migrants are arriving. Today looks like spring: the sky is clear and the sun is shining. A three-quarter moon floats above in the blue eastern sea. But the temperature is barely above freezing. In the woods, snow still clings to the trees in little patches in the crotches of north-facing branches. My breath hangs lightly ahead of me as I climb the hill to the northern meadow.

On the way up, the flicker flushes ahead of me. I walk into the meadow carelessly. A large hawk or owl flies up and away, too quickly and obliquely to identify. Embarrassed, I hope that, through inattention, I didn't chase away what I came to see.

For my goal this evening is, again, owls. I hope to see the short-eared owls, of course. But Meg Scanlon has reported seeing a pair of great horned owls close by. Just hearing them would make my day. The barred owl would, too. So I stand at the edge of the woods, quietly and hopefully. A man walks down the middle of the meadow with his dog. Nuthatches rasp in the distance and a jay fools me with its hawk imitation for a while. Chickadees pass through, hunting in the branches. Otherwise, the evening is very quiet. Again, no owls.

I'm really ready for spring!

March

Spring at last—perhaps

January stormed in, ages ago,
stiff-fingered and shivering, sat
and sat on the doorstep, left
a two-foot drift behind.

February stalked in then,
skeletal and hacking,
rattled sleet against the window,
bit us if we stepped outside.

Northeast winds hurled March at us,
chased ragged clouds in tatters by,
flung frozen rain at robins
puffed up on icy branches.

So went the days in chilly grays
while we all watched for spring,
and dreamed of it,
and fidgeted and waited.

At last a warm south wind crept in
with a dawn of treetop serenades
to make a feathered lady blush.
I, laughing, flung my hat

northward with the wind. And though
the flirtations of fifty-two springs—
they've kissed and skipped away—
have left me bruised and wiser, still,

if the rills that dance
in white ribbons today
are bewitched overnight
to pillars of ice

I'll stand, nonetheless, at dawn
like the doe who waits by the road,
ears up, eyes wide, huffing and stamping
first one hoof, then the other.

March 1

On this exuberant morning, I nearly leap with eagerness for spring. Two days ago, the first grackle appeared at the bird feeder. Today, the sky is blue and bright. But the temperature is only 24°; my breath smokes away into the early sunshine. My footsteps over crusty snow on brittle leaves echo down the little woodland valley. The streamlet hurries just as noisily down the Braille Trail toward the pond, bubbling as it runs beneath a roof of most exotic ice. New, quick-frozen ice it is, of spires and spears all interlaced in crystalline sparkling sheets. Thin, still-fragile ice it is, so clear the bubbles flow amoeba-like beneath to make of it a moving artistry. And where the waters run too fast and free for even such a flimsy corselet, scalloped openings remain to let them ripple unrestrained.

Winter holds the woodland yet, but feebly. Purple cowls of skunk cabbage poke through the dry brown leaves along the streamlet's banks. As I walk up the hillside, a kinglet flits in the naked canopy above. The woods ring with the mating calls of titmice and chickadees. At the border of woodland and meadow, the range wars of the titmice rage in feathery flutters and chases. Last month, those same gray birds hunted the treetops and bushes together, but now testosterone flows much like the waters in the valley. A red-bellied woodpecker taps at a tree, then carries some prize to a second woodpecker that sits quietly on a branch. The two fly away together.

Winter holds the woodland still, but it has glanced nervously over its shoulder and that, for the birds, suffices. This is the permanent residents' moment—the lull before the hordes of southern migrants arrive. They've shivered through the lean season, scorned the easy bugs of Louisiana for this: first choice of nesting site and the fattest hunting ground. And so the morning rings with their mating songs and flashes with their colors.

An oxymoron—a skinny woodchuck—appears abruptly, then strolls through the mature woods toward the second growth nearby. What will it find to eat so early in the year? Where did it come from? The second question is easily answered. Woodchuck footprints climb from a frozen, snowy hole, then trail off into the underbrush.

But I don't follow, so I still can't answer the first question. Instead, I hike back down to the pond to see what might be happening there. It's still frozen. The cattails still rattle listlessly. I hear white-throated sparrows, then see them. Still in a flock, they scratch in the snow and leaves beneath the brambles. Song sparrows join them, both in song and search. I suppose the white-throated flock will go north soon, but the song sparrows will probably stay.

I decide to go north, too, but only a little way. I wonder how early spring looks on the upper meadow.

It looks like robins.

Robins! Everywhere I look, I see robins—scolding from the treetops, swinging on the mullein, scratching in the woodland leaf mould, scouring the meadow, peering at me sideways from a twig above my head. I count them as residents. They could be Canadians, though, who wintered here and now loudly contemplate their journey on the next Northern Express. They could be early arrivals from the south, raucously reliving their journeys. I can't ask, and they don't tell.

No question about the red-winged blackbirds whirring in the meadow. They're early arrivals, tough enough to survive—no, to rejoice through—the last icy blows of winter.

I think that these early arrivals haven't flown far. Grackles, red-winged blackbirds, and turkey vultures winter in the southern states and so only have to cross a state or two to reach Pennsylvania. Of course, the advantage of arriving early is the same as for the permanent residents: the early bird...

The golden morning falls on a flock of cedar waxwings in the bittersweet. They're familiar winter residents, soon to fly north, but their colors seem sharper, their contours smoother. They flash red and yellow in the sunlight. I think they've just finished the spring molt and are dressed up for the dance.

And when a bluebird alights on a green pole in the sunlight in the middle of the meadow, breath stops. So, they say, Marilyn Monroe stopped hearts when she entered a room. But the bird seems unaware of himself. He flutters his feathers into place, settles down, and peers about. There is a wriggle in the grass. He drops upon it, returns to his perch, and sings. Some say the bluebird has no song, but he does. It's just a brief warble, but it's lovely. Perhaps any song would be lost to his utter, breathtaking blueness. Marilyn sang too, but who remembers?

March 6-7

After several days with temperatures in the teens, a strong south wind has blown milder, grayer days into Pennsylvania. On Thursday, the little stream's ice artistry had dripped to rounded rims of ice at the edges of the eddies; today, its palette holds just water, rippling and bubbling. The skunk cabbage cowls at its edges have pushed out of the earth and into business.

The pond, though, is still half covered by ice. Two Canada geese seem to be setting up a household on the marshy end. Four mallard drakes and a hen dashed about at the other end, or sat on the ice and watched.

Now that I have hearing aids, I can once again hear the high-pitched call of starlings. I'd forgotten how eerie it sounds. A downy woodpecker taps loudly high on a bare, dead stump. He seems to be drumming, rather than hunting, and there is a hole in a nearby branch. Two song sparrows rustle in the grasses among the cattails. Both mornings have been loud with the songs of red-winged blackbirds, robins, cardinals, white-throated sparrows, titmice, geese, jays, and doves. Well, probably doves; though barred owls also make a cooing sound.

On hearing aids. A couple of years ago, I realized that I couldn't hear the spring peepers with my left ear. Later, during a bird count, I realized that I'd also lost the ability to locate birds by sound. That's rather like losing three-dimensional vision. Subsequently, I noticed that I couldn't hear waxwings, crickets, and my wife's softer registers. Danger lurked in that latter loss. So in September, I bought a pair of digital hearing aids. The return of the peepers was more than the recovery of a lost song; it was the return of spring—both mine and the world's. Though I know I must lose the peepers sometime, at least I haven't yet.

Six jays seem to be mobbing something in the low area around the pond, but I can't see what they're shrieking at. The owls come to mind, of course. In any case, the jays are certainly exercised about something, and restlessly swoop from treetop to treetop, screaming as they fly. When they do land, they bounce on the branches so wildly that the trees shake.

I leave them clamoring below as I climb the hill to the northern meadow. But as I stand quietly at the edge of the woods, they appear again, still in a fairly tight group, still raising the dead, or at least trying. They aren't interested in me. Indeed, it seems like this is an internal issue. I suspect that one in that group is a female in heat.

In the line of bushes and small trees that bisects the meadow from east to west, one large tree—a sycamore—stands out. It seems to be a favorite perch. After the jays have finished rattling its twigs, a pair of bluebirds arrive to look around from its eastern branches and a sparrow of some sort *("sparrows of some sort" are also known to birders as LBJs: Little Brown Jobs*) sits in the west. When the bluebirds leave, a mockingbird takes their place. It sits quietly, and watches. His mating must be later. When the mockingbird has left, a male red-winged blackbird arrives, noisily. His mating season is now! The sun breaks through to ignite his bright red shoulders as he spreads his wings wide and sings. He must seem vast, strong, and virile to his more muted counterpart who has to be watching, unseen, among the brambles. Excuse me. Counterparts. He will be gathering a harem.

A doe nibbles her way up the hillside, then slowly and quietly disappears over the edge of the hill. After a while, I slip off, too.

March 13

It's early morning, and it's noisy. At the edge of the lower meadow, either a flicker or a pileated woodpecker is rattling the windows of dawn. Crows are mobbing something across the valley. I wonder if a great horned owl is the object of their attention, and maybe it is. But a large red-tailed hawk rows powerfully out of the melee and lands in the tree next to me. The crows keep hammering away across the valley, so perhaps the hawk silently thanked the owl and slipped away. It doesn't seem to be in a hurry, and no crows have followed it. It looks around for a bit, then floats across the meadow and north.

I'm still amazed by the repertoire of titmice. The one that owns the titmouse title to this corner of the woods is flitting from tree to tree, regaling all other titmice— and, incidentally, me—with his complete works. The folks at the Cornell School of Ornithology really ought to arrange a recording session with this guy. I think he would shame some who are proud of their prowess in bird call identification.

Of course, there are downy woodpecker and red-bellied woodpecker titles to the same corner, and those co-owners are rattling, tapping, and quirring in the trees above, oblivious to the titmouse and me.

A fox squirrel isn't so nonchalant about my presence. She dances tenuously on three or four twigs of a small bush, flipping her tail at me and chattering. The whole bush shakes, and it seems that she must fall off. I feign indifference and, after a bit, she jumps to the base of a large oak, intending, probably, to be off about her business. But another squirrel has come quietly from another tree to hers. Before she can catch her breath, he chases her up and around her oak. I understand that, among squirrels, this is considered foreplay. So as they chase each other through the oaks, I slip off to find the woodpecker.

I disturb four deer that have been browsing out of sight in a little hollow. They bound away, flags flying. And the woodpecker stops calling. But the crows are loud, once again, on the wooded hillside that falls from the upper meadow, so I cross the road, climb that hill—and find myself in a very different world.

Often, it seems, my walks turn sharp corners onto unexpected streets. So today—I have just stepped from the rambunctiousness of the mating game into a woods dark with hatred. The crows have found an owl. They swirl above a pair of spruce trees, a black cyclone of invective. More are coming, in twos and threes, from all directions, braying harsh encouragement. Like water down a bathtub drain, they curl in and drop into the surrounding trees. The trees bristle with crows, bouncing the boughs with their tantrums, leaping into the sky in spasms of rage, pouring waves of epithets into the saturated air. I cease to believe in birdsong—there only is, there only has ever been, the cacophony of crows. Yet now and then, barely audible in the tumult, there is a soft cooing, as of doves. But this comes from no dove. It is the low mutter of the cornered tiger. It is counterpoint to the crows' impotent fury. It reminds them that the sun does not always shine, that dusk comes, and with it, retribution.

I've seen many mobbings, but I've never sat in the middle of one before, and three observations surprise me. First, the crows, not the owl, do the clicking. Second, there are periods of absolute silence, as if all the crows are catching their breath at the same time. Perhaps even this cyclone has an eye. Finally, this drama didn't end in any climax I could see. It just dwindled to nothing. The crows just leaked away as though they'd forgotten why they were there.

Finally, the silence of gentle sounds: the whistle of a titmouse, the bubbling of a stream below. Though I'm so very close, I still haven't seen the owl. I circle the spruce trees for a better vantage point and—silently, suddenly, the large brown barred owl floats off toward the pines at the other end of the woods.

The crows see it, too, and now the hounds are back on the trail. This time, a blue jay tags along, rather like a puppy yipping from the tail of the pack. The chase leads across the woods, settles at the other end for a while, then returns. Crows swoop at the owl as it flies over me and back into the spruce. Once again, I'm in the middle of mayhem. Blinded by their passions, neither the crows nor the owl note my passing as I leak away.

March 15

The sycamore tree in the middle of the meadow sags with blackbirds. Suddenly, the flock pours like hot coffee into the meadow below. The tree springs back up; the meadow groans.

I'm soaking up sunshine under the naked apple tree beside the windmill. Song sparrows surround me. These are shy and obviously don't care to be stared at. Nonetheless, I stare. They flit through the lower branches of low bushes, scratch in the leaves, preen among the thorns of multiflora rose, and sing from a bough. It might be Eden. So goes life before the kids arrive.

And there's the problem: this imperative that bubbles up inside, boils, builds to bursting—to have those kids. The meadow buzzes with it—my first impression is that all the chicks will be blackbirds—but one bluebird's warble bobs above the sea of blackbird trills. A female in muted blue sits on a nest box, flutters to a nearby thistle head, then on to another and another until, at last, she perches by the bluest-of-blue singers. He must be saying what she wants to hear. And so goes Eden.

Were there crows in Eden? And if there were, did they lose their melodies to the apple? What did they do to deserve these rasps and rattles? Their vocal cords must be made from metal files and broken glass. The usual distant mayhem creeps closer, until finally a red-tailed hawk floats silently across the treetops, over the meadow, and into the woods on the other side. A ragged phalanx of obsidian arrows trails behind. And as the flight of black harpies passes, the obscenities they scream wash like waves across the brown grasses.

Then there is silence, relatively speaking.

For all morning, a flicker has jack-hammered the air with its ratchety ratchety call. The pileated woodpecker's call is similar, so I decide to see who really is making all that noise. For ten or fifteen minutes, he leads me on, from tree to tree, always just out of sight. At last I see his white rump leaving. And where he lands. I chuckle the hunter's joy as he shows at last his spotted breast, crimson crescent, and black moustache.

I think one never dares believe he hunts alone. Big hawks prey on little hawks, and eagles on the big. Above me, the hawk floats in lazy circles, gazing down. He (or she) is beautiful: white against the sky but for black wing markings and brown waistband. It sees me, certainly, but I'm too big to eat, and empty-handed. Good for me that I'm my size. Otherwise, I'd doubtlessly be breakfast, or tagging along, shrieking, with the crows.

April

The Price of Spring

A once-abode of eagles
is now upon its back
among the leaves
of last year's fall.

Its toes are in the air,
limbs lie loose and scattered
like old bones. Its tough old trunk
is mossy-green and gnawed
relentlessly by pale-white shelves.
They've nibbled branches back
to rich brown earth
that bright green spears
of spring thrust through

and I am teetering
between grief and wonder
on the fuzzy line where
death ends and life begins.

April 2

Lamb isn't in style this spring. March came in like a lion and went out...still snarling. After two weeks of snow and cold rain, today is supposed to be a warm and sunny break before more cold rain. But so far, it's cold, gray and damp.

The air above the pond is saturated, surely, but with birdsong as well as with vapor. Cardinals, robins, jays, red-winged blackbirds, and a towhee, I think, though I don't see him. It takes me a while to get used to the voices of the spring arrivals. A goose sits on the still surface; two others stand in the grass. The three are motionless; they could be decoys. After a few minutes, the two stoop to nibble grass and preen. The guard drifts—it seems—my way. Suddenly, a fourth barrels over, horn blaring. It circles. My three honk back, three-fold louder. Their heads bob on their long necks—to squeeze out every last decibel, I suppose. Mayhem reigns for a long minute. I don't know what this is about, but the fourth flies off.

The "guard" goose goes off duty to guzzle in the muck. It looks like a headless mound of feathers floating on the water, a refugee, perhaps, from a pillow factory. It pops back up, raises its head to the full length of that neck, and looks around. Something long, thin, and limp hangs from both sides of its bill. Before it swallows, it inspects me with a sidelong, proprietary glare. I assure it that I don't want whatever it has.

A kingfisher rattles over. It lands on a dead finger of a tree that once overlooked the pond, but now has mostly tumbled in. The bird fishes carefully: its head swivels about in quick jerks, left, right, into the water, up to the sky. This seems strange to me for a moment. After all, it can't be easy to interpret the subtle shadows that dart and drift beneath the pond's glitter. Blue herons, as they fish, stand quite still. Never have I seen one look up. But the herons are bigger than the sharpshinned hawk that patrols the pond at times. Suddenly, the kingfisher swoops out over the water, dives headlong in, and emerges with something brown and limp hanging from its bill. Back on the limb, it gives the thing a shake, then flings it back into the water and rattles to a perch across the pond. I suppose that the old rhyme about Jack Sprat also applies to kingfishers, geese, and long thin things in the water.

The mirror is dimpled with little circles, so I put my raincoat on. I was cold, anyway. Now I'm a little less cold. A little flock of chickadees lands above me among the elm buds. A cardinal, bright red framed by the feathery green of a rose bush, whistles the traditional tune, but with a syncopation at the end that's new to me. Lovely!

Less musical, but just as delightful, is a buzzing in the distance. I think the chipping sparrows have returned.

I'm still cold, so I walk up the hill toward the upper meadow. The songs change to those of song sparrows, titmice, the flicker, and maybe a Carolina wren. Everywhere—in the marsh, on the floor of the woods, in the meadow—green spears thrust out of the earth and into whatever the air has to offer. Today, that seems like an act of great faith.

Soon I'm shivering by a familiar tree at the edge of the meadow to watch whatever may unfold. Robins scold from the line of bushes and trees in the center of the meadow. Red-winged blackbirds sing and display. The tree swallows are back! At first, they're just perched, fluffed up and quiet, on the bird boxes. But as the morning warms, they flutter off and up, up, until, a hundred feet or so above me, they swoop in breathtaking dives to millimeters above the ragged brown meadow. They dip and dart across the goldenrod and grass at military speeds, then flutter up again for altitude to do it all again. I still can't imagine that bugs would be active in this cold, but the swallows must know what they're doing. I'm learning that what I can or can't imagine has little to do with anything.

Over in the sycamore, the mockingbird has warmed up. His liquid medley pours across the meadow. It has a hodgepodge loveliness, reminiscent of a patchwork quilt. It's surely territorial and therefore, as far as I can tell, sung solely for other mockingbirds. Sure, I'm delighted and amused, but the bluebirds and blackbirds are simply going about their own business. If they're listening, it doesn't show. But he knows, and I know, that, scattered about the meadow and the woods, others of his kind are listening carefully and are impressed, or unimpressed, by the length or volume or diversity of his song. Judging from the kingliness of his perch, his song must be impressive.

Suddenly, the staccato pop pop pop of small arms practice at the police firing range punctures my mood. My world has awakened—the one with predators I'm not immune to. Small arms are followed by the shrill beep beep of a "construction" vehicle backing up somewhere in the distance—"construction" or "destruction", depending on which side of the bulldozer's blade you're on. A new noise, from a cement saw or wood chipper, I'd guess, rips at the air that the swallows slice more cleanly and quietly through.

It's time to leave. As I walk from meadow to woods, a Carolina wren peers down at me from the branches. The flicker scalloping away, white tail flashing, reminds me of an upside down deer in flight. But I'm the one who is fleeing.

April 7

Perhaps we'll find the lamb in April. The sun is shining through a high cirrus ceiling, the temperature is in the fifties, and an insistent wind from the Gulf of Mexico wants to take my hat to Hudson's Bay.

The woods are turning fuzzy green. Multiflora rose, viburnum, and the many still-anonymous bushes are pushing feathery young leaves out of hard brown twigs. Magicians pretend to do that sort of thing; plants really do it. The leaf-strewn floor is busy with robins, a titmouse, and a chipmunk that doesn't like my appearance. He rattles at me for minutes, then leaps away in haste from tree trunk to tree trunk, probably to tattle.

For all this, the woods would be quiet, were it not for the woodpeckers. A red-bellied woodpecker has been quirring in the area for a while, but now he's found a deep resonance in a tall tree and is drumming. He hammers vigorously, sends a hollow staccato booming across the woods, then waits. In moments, its echo rolls back from some other outlook across the hill. He hammers and listens, hammers and listens, and I feel that I'm at one end of a game of ping pong in the trees. "Game" may be a weak word for it—I suspect that a female is listening very critically.

I don't know how they make so much noise with those wicked bills without tearing the trees apart. When so inclined, they chisel quite large holes without making much noise at all. Yet drumming doesn't seem to leave chips or a hole. I suppose that, had I been born with the equipment, I'd know how to use it.

Gift-giving and the chase will come later for the big woodpecker. A pair of downy woodpeckers have reached the prenuptial—or maybe the nuptial—stage. Quick movement high above betrays a quiet, determined chase through the treetops. The female darts from tree to tree, waiting for the male to land a few feet above her before dashing off to the next. He follows, only wing beats behind. His bright red cockade flashes as he flies. At this distance, the male's red patch is usually only visible through binoculars, but I hardly need them to see it today. It's ruffled up and blazing like a bad hair day. But I don't think he's going to have a bad day.

Their mating dance swings through the trees and up the hill, out of sight. I follow, more slowly, less quietly, and a lot less excitedly. Oh, I'm eager to see what's happening on the meadow, but, well, we all know the difference between watching and doing.

Someone has mowed a broad strip down the length of the meadow. The birds seem pleased: the strip is prowled by four species of hunters. Their objectives are the same—insects shorn of their vegetable rooftop—but the hunting styles are very different. Starlings waddle in loose military ranks, snapping up whatever hops or runs in front of their march. Robins forego such group effort; each stands alone, motionless and listening until, suddenly, it darts and spears some small creature that rustled too loudly at the wrong time. Bluebirds sit on the nest boxes, peering about. Sometimes they flutter out and back, like flycatchers, after flying prey; sometimes they drop to the ground to catch something there. Tree swallows swoop like scythes upon whatever flits just above the grass.

One swallow, though, is perched at the doorway of a nest box, furtively peering and poking into the hole. After a minute or two, she looks about, flutters off to the hunt, and a second immediately appears, all nonchalance, to alight on the roof. The theory seems to be that the swallow is quicker than the eye: "actually, there's only one swallow, and he's just resting from the hunt. There's nothing at all of interest in the nest box. Really, there isn't."

Two men with a pickup truck are busily putting up new bird boxes. I hadn't known if these boxes were checked and changed. It's good that they are. But I wonder at the absence of predator guards beneath the boxes. Last year in a nest box at Bayer Corp., we found a snake curled up and happily digesting the chickadee eggs we'd been counting, day by day. The predator guard was loose. We left the snake alone—snakes have to eat, too. But we rushed to inspect the guards on all the other boxes. We didn't intend to run a delicatessen.

I turn a bit too quickly at the clink clink clink of the hammer as a new pole goes into the ground. Two deer snort and huff behind me—we hadn't seen each other.

87

They leap away in a brief pas de deux, their white skirts flying. But I've gone suddenly catatonic. Maybe I was just their imagination. They resume browsing and, after a while, dissolve into a thicket.

It's time for my dinner. Past time, really. So I walk quickly and rather noisily through the woods. Two robins that had been hunting among the leaves flush ahead of me. Robins? No, thrushes! Dinner? No, thrushes! I follow them through the undergrowth. They seem to be a pair: they always flush together and stay pretty close. I think I see their nest. But I can't tell what kind of thrushes they are: gray overall, with no apparent eye ring, and rather heavily spotted. Maybe gray-cheeked thrushes? That's hard to believe. I don't think these are headed north. Then I see a rufus tail as they lead this annoying paparazzi one more bush away from the nest. Hermit thrushes, maybe? I'll come back to listen to the morning songs. But now, I'm really late for dinner.

Alas, the birds won't let me go. Down the hill at the edge of the marshy meadow, a Carolina wren sings from the bushes. I can't quite find him. And there is a…tree sparrow? But I can't quite see the spot on his breast. Finally, he turns. Tree sparrow. And a towhee is trilling from a low branch nearby. I have to listen for just a moment…

Oh yes, dinner. When I was a teen, fishing sometimes erased the clockmarks from my day. I would find myself hastening up the hillside at sunset with a family rule echoing in my head. "Dinner is at 6:30. Absentees fend for themselves." Forty years later, a bald guy with hearing aids and glasses still rushes off the hillside with the setting sun behind, and angst ahead.

April 10

I'm hiking up the thrushes' hill just as the sun rises above the eastern line of trees. Perhaps the thrush will sing at morning? Everyone else is. The air is clear to the eye, but a vegetable soup of themes to the ear, rather like a symphony orchestra warming up. Carolina wrens, titmice, cardinals, red-winged blackbirds, jays…those are the ones I can identify. But I don't hear the silver splashes of thrush-song.

As I approach the bushy area where I first saw the thrushes, I see a glimmer of one leaving. "Hermit" seems a most appropriate name. Long cold minutes pass. I walk the wet leaves quietly, then stand beside another tree and watch. The "thrushes' nest" I thought I saw last time is really a blue jay nest. The pair of jays have been furtively in and out of their tangle of grape and rose vines several times; now they fuss—uncharacteristically quietly for jays—at me as I pass too closely. I bow to their greater comfort by finding a watching spot farther away.

The voices of towhees, chickadees, a flicker, and a red-bellied woodpecker filter through the woods and, one by one, their embodiments follow. Not so, the thrushes, though. I give up on them…for today.

A quick check of the meadow shows the air full of wheeling tree swallows. Swallows and bluebirds are scattered on nest boxes as far as I can see. Blackbirds sing from the trees at the meadow's edge.

I can no longer see my breath. Indeed, the warmth of the sun is ever more beguiling. A robin sits on a sunlit branch, tootling and cheerioing. I drift sleepily down the hill toward the pond. Suddenly, something that sounds a bit like a cat is above me. It reminds me of a catbird, but not quite—or a jay, but not quite that, either. I'm awake now. And right above my head, climbing headfirst down a grapevine, is a red-breasted nuthatch! What a raspy, funny sound to come out of such a small bird. It hangs upside down and says it again.

At the base of the hill, I'm puzzled again by that "tree sparrow." He won't pose as I wish, but as I strain to look at him, a female cardinal hauls a stem of grass twice her length into the brambles. A brown creeper scrambles up the tree beside me. So we're even: the sparrow keeps his anonymity, I am twice blessed. A Carolina wren sings "doodly doodly doodly" from somewhere in a tall white pine. I crane my neck and peer into the tree from several angles, to no avail. But one of those angles delights me with the wheeling roller coaster flight of a barn swallow. I'm reminded of that adage from kindergarten, "Accept gifts; say thank you; don't grab."

The willows' yellow-green tresses sway gently over the pond. A pair of geese float in the middle; a wood duck slips along the edge. He fixes me in one bright red eye, then leaps into the air in a dazzling spray. Whoever named this duck faced a dilemma: to highlight its backwoods habits or its exotic plumage. That namer must have been a humble soul. And so a duck that nests in trees, but looks like he might have been bred to please the emperor of China, is just a "wood duck." Farther out, a mallard drake drifts quietly, guzzling green pastures just below the surface. His orange legs flash behind him, his dark green head glistens with beads of water in the bright sun. A ruby-crowned kinglet flits from twig to branch in the bushes.

He's small and modest till a ray of sun ignites his cap. Ruby-crowned, indeed! "Crowned with fire" would be more apt. Yet even in such company, the emperor's eye would fall first on the wood duck.

Tadpoles wriggle from the filmy green pond bottom to make circles at the top. And just beyond them, two painted turtles dance. Were they man and woman, you would say they waltzed. Floating green nose to green nose, their yellow stripes drawing one long line, the larger one swims slowly forward, the smaller slowly back. Their rear feet paddle gently in unison, their front stretch wide as if to hug. Now and then, the smaller gently pats the larger on the right cheek, then the left. If the smaller is the male, as the field guide suggests, he leads her with those gentle pats from the fallen spruce out to a deeper place. And there they turn together and descend into the darkness of the bedroom below.

"Cold-blooded" seems a misnomer. Rather, "as warm as the waters allow."

At the pond's inlet, the cattails are a forest of naked shafts tipped with ragged brown tufts. They nod solemnly with the breezes. To them, it might still be November. But a goldfinch arrives, bright yellow and obsidian against their somber tans. A buzzy call floats up from somewhere in their ranks, either swamp sparrow or chipping sparrow.   In either case, they're back. And at the cattails' bases, all around, their replacements are arriving. They're bright green spears, six inches tall.

The skunk cabbages have begun to send up broad green leaves. Soon the business side of photosynthesis will shove the reproductive side, face down, into the mud.

A little brown vole scurries from one clump of grass to the next. Well that he vanishes quickly; minutes ago, a red-tailed hawk circled us, low and slow.

April 16

Death isn't the subject I'd choose to contemplate on a bright spring morning. Perhaps I'd never choose it. Death volunteers.

I'm standing quietly beside an old oak at the edge of the southern meadow. Cardinals, titmice, and towhees are conducting the morning census: loudest are those whose territories I'm standing in, less so are their counterparts on the adjacent lots, and those farther still are very faint. A fox squirrel is scrambling about in the high reaches of the nearby trees, nibbling buds, I presume.

Directly above me, draped all through the oak's upper branches, are the tendrils and tentacles of a grapevine. It has so enveloped the oak that it's surprising that the oak has survived. Indeed, many don't, so I've been asked to cut the vines that seem most threatening. Occasionally, I do. I cut this one in early winter. It's a tough old ropy snake of a creature a couple of inches thick. In January, it was just dry lumber. The sawdust sifted to the snow below, a dry, lifeless powder. But now, spring has called the juices from below. And now, the stump bleeds glistening drops of its life onto the leaf rubble below. Oak leaf rubble. Perhaps the oak will thrive again. One lives, one dies, and I decided which. The wisdom of this choice is doubtlessly trivial. But it's a microcosm of the human dilemma. Our choices are seldom whether something dies, but rather, which one.

As I walk quietly down the hill, a red-tailed hawk floats from high in the oak over the same path I'm taking. A chipmunk hiding under a barberry bush shifts its weight. I hadn't seen it before. Now I look back into a tiny unblinking black eye that's looking right at me. In the woods, at least, moving a muscle will betray you.

I stand motionlessly behind a chest-high fallen oak, green with moss and gnawed by fungi that are sucking it back into the earth it once towered over. After a few minutes, the squirrels and chipmunks reappear to scramble about the woods floor. Several turkeys stalk slowly up the hill among the skunk cabbage that line a rill. One walks directly toward me, poking about in the leaves. At last she raises her head and her small black eye is aimed at me. She studies me for a while, then resumes her foraging. Now, though, she's moving across the hillside away from me. Soon, she disappears into the rill's slight depression.

As her form blends into the skunk cabbage and woodland debris, a hawk's head appears from behind a fallen tree. It looks all around, its wings wide and fluttering. I think it's the red-tail from a few minutes ago, now covering and killing a fresh catch. Beneath the alert eyes and broad wings, steel talons squeeze and search for the vital point in some small creature. I once saw a sharp-shinned hawk kill and eat a starling. The process took over an hour. So, after five or ten minutes, I meander over to see what it's eating. Hawk and prey have gone without a trace. It seems likely that this kill went directly to the young in a high nest somewhere.

But even as the hawk killed, the chipmunk chattered at me from a log, two squirrels spiraled up and down an oak, and the birds sang on. In The Immense Journey, Loren Eiseley described a similar vision. He came upon a raven perched in the middle of a woodland glade, a nestling wriggling in its beak. The parents, then an assembly of other small birds, fluttered and protested from the bushes that ringed the vale, but the raven just gulped, then whetted its beak on the dead branch. There was a moment of silence. Then one small bird, and another, began to sing. Soon the vale rang with their songs. There, in the presence of the black bird that sits at the heart of life, the little birds chose to sing, for life is sweet and sunlight beautiful.

And all around me on my woodland hill, May apples, still furled like closed umbrellas, are poking out of the leaf duff. Winter has passed, the hunter is gone,

May is coming!

It's time for me to hike on, down the hill now, to look for it. The ground is squishy with the rains of the past few days. Water seeps from little ledges and runs down a multitude of rills to the stream below. That unnamed little creek gushes through the valley, pregnant with the spring rains. The skunk cabbages have finished with pollination. Now their broad leaves are bright green sails upon the waters that rush to the pond.

Above the pond, barn swallows swoop and dive. Two geese preen beside it. Frogs dive from the bank and sing from the cattails. Six painted turtles sprawl on half-sunken logs, soaking in sunshine. A red-winged blackbird shouts angrily at me from an overhanging branch; nearby, one of his mates must sit quietly on a low nest, waiting for her hero to chase me away. And out in the center of the pond, one green darner chases another out of his territory. Newly migrated from the south, the field guide says. I didn't know that dragonflies migrate, too.

DNA fingerprinting is expanding our view of the mating habits of many birds. It has long been known, for example, that red-winged blackbirds are polygynous: one male defends a territory and mates with as many females as the territory can support. Males with the best territories have the biggest harems. But life for the females may not be best in the richest territories, for the lower the female is in the harem's pecking order, the less help the male gives in raising the young. So it can be better to be one of a few in poorer territory. And the expanded view? DNA studies have shown that the male only fathers most of the chicks in his territory. It seems that, for the most part, this is due to excursions by the females, rather than incursions by other males. The older females seem to have more chicks by outside fathers.

Nature does so often mirror humanity.

April 19

Up the hill to the upper meadow I go, once again to hunt for the pair of thrushes. Rain has been predicted, and in the northwest, thunderheads are bulging into huge white towers. One has reached the high cold winds; it's flat-topped, anvil-shaped and powerful.

Down here, though, the sun shines on early spring beauty. Goldfinches nibble the buds of a red maple: black and gold on light green, framed in silver bark with a light blue-sky background. May apples here are dark green, wide open and three or four inches high. Bumblebees blunder clumsily across the air to dangle heavily from pink and white blossoms on an old, gnarled apple tree. This must have been an orchard, once. Now the apple tree has been half enveloped by grapevines. A house wren bubbles in the distance, then appears among the vines. A yellow-rumped warbler passes quietly among the goldfinches. The air is a banquet of birdsong, but the main dish is towhee. Loudly, persistently, from every direction: towhee. There's only one; there seem to be twenty. His song is complex, varied, and lovely, but what immoderation!

No thrushes, though. I give up on them for the day.

The old windmill in the meadow stands over newly mown grass. The mowing of the meadow is accomplished. My day might be accomplished, too. The northwest sky is dark and low.

Perhaps the oncoming storm lends the bittersweet loveliness of transience to the scene around me. Perhaps the futility of capturing such colors drove van Gogh mad. There is no palette with the bluebird's blue; there are surely no words to describe it. But the binoculars' circle paints a vision on my mind that may last long beyond the storm. In the center stands the dark green pole with the pine-brown bird house. The lower background is the light green shimmering meadow of new grass; the upper background, the darker green of new leaves on a tangle of bushes. On the house, the bird of ineffable blue and orange fire with his mate of safer, muted beauty. And here, maybe, lay van Gogh's doom: no gallery can capture artistry like this. It moves. It flashes as the bluebirds flutter to the grass and back. Like knives, dark blue-green above, pure white below, swallows slash across the canvas. In the wild maze of the bushes, as two blackbirds raise their wings to sing, obsidian ignites in crimson and yellow flame. And finally, in a moment of utter visual and biological whimsy, two white butterflies zig and zag a drunken dance across the field. So fragile, they seem, yet unconcerned. As though a tiny tornado captures them, they whirl together in a flickering pirouette at the very center of the avian stage. But this is where they live and flaunting white capes at birds is what they do: they exit the circle untouched and whole.

From some hidden perch, a mockingbird plays Greek chorus with his cacophony of squeaks, shrieks, and trills, lest I take all this too seriously. I must seem a little dense, for a pink-billed field sparrow lands near my head and adds his ping pong tune.

April 24

Late April, but my breath floats ahead of me on January air! The temperature now is 30°. The multiflora rose leaves are frosted and limp. Garlic mustard stands in penitent congregations, bowing to an angry god. The skunk cabbages have lowered their sails; they drooped in the night chills and now hang floppily like the dead sheets of an unmanned frigate.

The pond lies still and steamy. A pair of wood ducks slide away to vanish among the cattails. For a moment, they seem to swim upon a pan of water that steams quietly just before boiling. But, of course, the pond's long frosty exhalation is far closer to ice than steam. Near the center, on the grating of the outlet drain, the goose has built her nest. At first, her head is tucked beneath her wing. She sleeps…well, maybe not. The binoculars show one black eye staring right back into mine. The gander has been quietly sitting nearby on the shore. As the sun rises over the hills, he paddles to the other side to sit where new sunshine falls at the cattails' feet. The female idly tucks escaped sticks and grass back into the nest. Now, done with the morning tidying up, she stretches her long neck and lays her head flat on the edge of the drain. She looks bored. Perhaps she wishes I would do something interesting. I suspect that she knows she could handle me quite easily, should I need handling.

The air above the pond is cold, but not quiet. A female flicker alights in a tree across the pond, to the rattle of a male close by. A titmouse calls loudly from just above my head. Two blue herons fly high above, south to north. As the morning warms, the chorus grows: Carolina wrens, towhees, red-winged blackbirds…the usual singers of an April day.

But there's a yellow flash among a rosebush's thorns! A male yellow warbler pops out, then quickly disappears again. "Phoebe" floats down from the barn, and there he is, fluttering under the eaves. As I climb the hill toward the meadow, a house wren warbles from the bushes and barn swallows flutter above. A second dawning, this time in my head: these are the vanguard of the main migration! The long-distance flyers, the insect eaters: warblers, orioles, flycatchers, vireos, and so many others are arriving! Most cross the Gulf between April 10 and May 10. The cross-country passage to Pennsylvania usually takes about ten days more. And here they are!

Whole species left last fall with nothing but new feathers, a store of fat, some gathered wisdom, and messages hidden in their DNA to keep their kind from extinction. They return now to turn those gifts into a new generation, and with but a brief summer to do it in. They flow north as a tide rising, driven, not by the masses of sun and moon, but by the hand that moves the stars themselves.

The vanguard, however, has a lesson to teach about risk and reward. We tend to lionize pioneers. That's reasonable, for fame and fortune often fall to the first to get there—wherever "there" may be. But the warbler shivering in the multiflora rose could tell the other side of the old adage: the early bird might also freeze.

May

Frogs

There's some slow rhythm of the soul,
urgent as the labors of the heart,
but seasonal, akin to morning wakenings,
that calls me pondside in the night
in May to hear the eager songs.

In the middle of an aria
I tiptoe in--
all goes quiet, nonetheless.
But passion quickly subdues caution:
one by one the singers join
in syncopated choruses
of lusty trills and bass profundos

that pluck, somehow,
some deep genetic chords--
in me. I stand enraptured
by an unseen choir, laughing
with the wild untutored cadences--

though this year I have found,
while spring is strong in my right ear,
winter still lies deep upon my left.
So frost creeps slowly in, I guess.
For now, I simply turn
my good side to the songs,
sigh, and smile again.

Next year, and next again,
will find new singers,
new listeners on the shore,
but the old, old songs
and the ancient joy.

May 1

I'm late. The sun is up, the birds are up, and I'm just arriving. The morning is cold (45°), damp, and thick cloud cover is moving in. But the birds don't seem to care. As I walk up the hill from the stream valley, the songs of red-winged blackbirds, towhees, and chickadees float behind me. A heron flies over, south to north, just as it did last week. There must be a heron roost south of Latodami. It would be worth looking for. Years ago I saw such a nesting site in a row of rather small trees by a stream near Logan, Utah: silhouettes of dozens of gangling four-foot-tall birds standing about on large, rough nests perched atop twenty-foot trees. It conjured an image of a bunch of teenagers hanging out on top of a hedge.

Now, though, I stand under an oak, with May apples and garlic mustard all around my feet. The sun is still low enough to shine beneath the cloud cover. I appreciate the warmth, and nearby, in the crotch of another oak, a large coon seems appreciative, too. At first, it lay with its back to the sun—and to me. Now it has turned a bit to catch the sun on its broad left shoulder and to blink lazily at me.

The sun's gold turns gray and a chill falls over me. The sun has risen above the clouds, and March is back. Two titmice flit along a high road, treetop to treetop. I follow them in the binoculars, wondering whether they're a pair or if this is a turf battle. Their road runs through that nearby oak, and suddenly I'm looking right into the eyes of the coon. We're both startled. I look away quickly. "I know you just stepped out of the shower, but really, I didn't see a thing." She knows better. Slowly, casually, she climbs twenty feet higher to a place where leaves screen her from my rudeness. I think she just closed her blinds.

Down the hill, now, to the cadences of a red-bellied woodpecker and a flicker. Below, dogwoods are blossoming radiant white against the newly greening wood.

The clouds have thinned. The sun breaks through to land on the bright green of ferns awakening from the brown leaves. Most are spindly, with fiddleheads in lumpy balls—scraggly teenagers, just getting up. But those that are fully awake are lovely, delicate green lace. There are two kinds, Christmas fern and a twice-cut species.

The ferns are arriving; the skunk cabbages seem to be leaving. The little stream's valley is a sea of green sails, but the sails are rent and ragged, as if they've seen a storm. Strong winds did sweep the area on Sunday, with very large hail. Perhaps the image is more appropriate than I had first thought.

The May apples don't seem so torn up, though. They do seem larger and more mature than those higher up the hillside. A scattering of a yellow daisy-like flower with purple buds and stem-clasping leaves appears among the skunk cabbage—but not in the field manual.

As I'm pondering the daisies, a rather wet and bedraggled gray and white cat emerges from the tangle of barberry bushes beside the path. It follows the path for a few yards, then vanishes again under the barberries. But not to all eyes. Three towhees flutter above the bushes, squeaking like rusty swings. (*Alarm calls are never melodic. They're usually scratchy or raspy. I've read that one characteristic of such sound patterns is that they're difficult to localize, and so protect the caller.*) They follow something unseen to me up the hill. At last, when their apparition has passed some boundary that is also invisible to me, they return quietly. One, apparently back on his rounds, sings above me, then across the stream, and up the hill.

Another, a female, flutters to a bare space beneath an oak and rustles among the leaves. Her hunt seems unique among the leaf duff hunters: whereas song sparrows and juncos, for example, scratch furiously as if running in place, then look around their feet for bugs, this towhee seems to scratch with both feet at once, hops backward and inspects her work from a little distance. Her approach seems more athletic and looks kind of funny, but it must be effective. She's fat and happy.

Earlier this year, during a quiet time, I poked among those same leaves. On the damp dark earth beneath lay a striped spider, an ant or two, and a pale thin many-legged creature that curled up in the light. Tiny brown ovals scuttled off into crevices and cracks. There's another world under there. I recognized some of the inhabitants: sow bugs and millipedes rowed away, with names. Most, though, slipped quickly from startled scrutiny into happy, invisible anonymity. The towhee surely knows them well—by taste, if not by name. She whistles while she works.

The clouds have thickened again. The chill is back, so I move on to find—a lone migrating shore bird at the pond. It's certainly headed for the larger lakes farther north. It's also certainly a sandpiper. Knee-high in the shallows, it probes the mud with a long bill. It runs, it bobs, it preens on the shore, but it doesn't fly. I've never seen a solitary sandpiper, but this may be one. It has the eye-ring and the yellow-green legs of that species, but unless it flies, I can't be sure. At last it leaves for the farther shore, white flashes from the sides of its tail, and it is officially a solitary sandpiper—a "life bird!" Ahh!

May 7

The air is heavy this morning, the sky a misty gray and prescient of rain. My head is heavy, too: full of some spring virus. But the trees are full of birds, so I don't care.

The edge of the upper meadow, just inside the woods, often seems to be a bird highway. If there were fast food franchises for birds, an elm on this highway would be one today. In the last few minutes, three Baltimore orioles, a female rose-breasted grosbeak, a yellow warbler, and a couple of titmice have stopped there to nip the new buds. The buds are at the very tips of the whippiest of tables, so such meals require some acrobatics. The larger birds stretch far out, swaying; the smaller ones often find themselves hanging upside down. I stand on big flat feet on the safe and solid earth, laughing.

Songs I know and songs I don't fill my ears. A flicker, a wren, and a pair of cardinals pass over. One oriole is stripping bark from a grapevine, probably for a nest nearby. This isn't far enough from a blue jay's nest, and on the oriole's third trip, the jay's patience ends. After a brief, but furious fluttering, the oriole flies away. Chickadees have been high in the elm, as well. Suddenly one darts through the branches faster than I've ever seen a chickadee fly, with a hummingbird at his tail. The air must be heavy with hormones, too. It's chasing time. Two of the orioles are more yellow than orange—yearlings, I suppose. The third is bright orange and certainly king: he chases both away and reigns in the elm. Oh, and he goes over to the grape vine to strip more bark, unmolested.

A new warbler arrives, high in the tree. Except for a hint of brown among the leaves, all I can see from below is a white belly and a needle beak. Before I can name him, he's gone. Sibley's next field guide should be entitled, <u>Birds Upside Down, Obscured by Leaves, and Moving</u>. It should be readable only when held above your head, and should come with a tube of liniment.

Out on the meadow underneath the windmill, a wren sits on a branch a few feet away, singing mightily. Somewhere in the line of bushes that splits the meadow, the mockingbird is whistling and rasping his outrageous medley. Above me, at the very top of the windmill, a bluebird is singing, too. In the dimmer light, he isn't as visually dazzling, so now I can concentrate on his melody—I wonder how the current crop of teen divas would sound if they sang in the dark. Anyway, before this year, I'd seldom heard a bluebird sing. Now I hear it often. That probably has more to do with my awareness than with the bluebirds' habits.

About half of the meadow on this side has faded from the vibrant green of mid-April to a sickly yellow-brown. I'd been forewarned, so I'm not alarmed. This section was sprayed with Roundup and will be plowed under soon. It's part of a program to wrest the meadow from the largely alien grasses and weeds that have invaded it and to reintroduce native grasses. The hope, I'm sure, is that native flora will attract and sustain more native fauna. The dying isn't easy to watch, but the cause surely seems right. The swallows and bluebirds aren't avoiding the dying area; the swallows may be favoring it. The bugs must feel naked there.

I was partly right. Jose Taracido of California University of Pennsylvania specializes in such projects and is in charge of this one. His method is to kill everything on a plot, replant with native grasses and wildflowers without plowing, then burn or cut the plot periodically. Native grasses like switchgrass and two species of bluestem form root masses that can crowd out the aliens, since the natives evolved with fire, close-cutting (well, chomping by bison, then), and undisturbed soil. The aliens thrive where people have disturbed the land. Since these grasses provide superior food and cover, he hopes a native upper meadow will attract meadowlarks, bobolinks, and sparrows that currently don't live here. I was surprised to learn that the 30-acre upper meadow is more likely to attract wildlife than is the 15-acre lower meadow. Bigger appears to be better.

The process should take two or three years.

The meadow is busy, but the woods are calling today. Just yards from the elm, the gray day is broken by the dazzling whiteness of a group of dogwoods in flower. Suddenly, silently, a scarlet tanager crystallizes from a moist breeze among the dogwood blossoms. The rest of the world falls out of focus as he stands, cardinal red and obsidian black on a sea of pure white, looking casually over his shoulder. He's the essence of beauty, unaware of itself. A minute passes—or maybe an hour. Too soon a breeze whisks him away, the glade exhales, and time moves on.

Gradually, the rest of the world comes back into focus. There's the bubbling song of a house wren. A pair of indigo buntings flies through. We're back. But, oh, the tanager!

And oh, the dogwoods! Look at them again. Their blossoms don't face willy-nilly everywhere. They present their pure white petals face up, as if with open hands, an offering to the sun, perhaps, and to the birds above. Surely to the heavens. And just as surely not to we who walk the soggy leaf-strewn earth. We see them backlit, like the shoulders of a bride, a beauty faced away. We're allowed to worship from a distance.

It's a privilege just to stand, in May, among the dogwoods.

May 13

The goose is sitting stoically on her nest, light rain beading on her bill. The willows' long tresses hang heavily, dripping and forlorn. Today they have reason to weep: the storm yesterday took one down completely and tore a large branch from another. Their leaves have just begun to wither.

But the raindrops lie like silver beads on the honeysuckle leaves and drip sparkling from every twig and leaf tip. Orioles are whistling, unconcerned, from the treetops. A bullfrog groans from somewhere among the foot-tall cattails on the bank nearby.

The little stream runs loudly away from the pond, nearly out of its banks. A catbird loudly claims the bushes all around. Caught between the exuberance of stream and bird, I can hear nothing else. Then there is a flash of yellow, and I forget the catbird, the stream, the rain. The nervous hunt of a prothonotary warbler is a rare and fragile vision. He's only a few yards away and quite intent upon the business of poking and peering among the new buds of the surrounding bushes. There is gray on his wings and white on his tail, but to me he's a study in bright yellow and sharp black eyes. I think those eyes miss little. He's also a study in agility: he dangles upside down, he leaps from a twig for a fluttering bug without condescending to unfold his wings. But most of all, warblers teach impermanence. In little darts and dashes, he vanishes downstream.

I squish up the hill toward the meadow, knee-high in wet grass. The catbird calls fade, to be replaced by those of towhees, wrens, blackbirds, and one I don't know. As is my wont, I stop at the edge of the woods, lean against a large cherry tree, and watch. Over the meadow, the sky has grown grayer; dusk has fallen beneath the trees. Leaves gleam in the dim light. The tree's skin is cool, wet, and muscular against my back—it's a little strange to lean on another living being, albeit (apparently) insentient. The aliens of science fiction are seldom odder than trees.

Rain rattles on the canopy, but isn't reaching me yet. As it begins to leak through, there is a constant fluttering of leaves as droplets collect on the uppermost, roll off the leaf tip to plunge onto a leaf below that shudders, bounces back, then droops as the droplet collects itself, runs to the tip, and falls again. Soon there is one rain beneath the canopy, another above. With a loud plap, a drop of the lower rain falls on my hat.

The pattering of droplets has grown into the staccato beats of massed snare drums. Faster, faster they fall, until my ears register only a wild static. The sky has darkened far beyond gray. Gusts of wind whip through the new leaves. I've

A chipmunk and me, in the rain

pulled the drawstrings on my raincoat tight and raised the hood. The rain is no longer falling; it's sweeping over us in sheets. Smooth-barked trees are slick and black. The shaggier have become disheveled hairy legs of giants. A robin flies by, low and fast. A chipmunk runs across my foot and disappears into a hole beside me. Two brownish warblers, too ruffled to identify, sit in an elm's lower branches. They seem stoic, not miserable. Now and then they shake off the rain, from head to tail feathers. My tree is breaking the wind and rain; still, water drips steadily and loudly onto my hood from some protuberance higher up the tree. I feel like I'm standing under a faulty faucet. But I haven't the heart to look up at it, and besides, everywhere else is wetter. Yet even as premature night is falling all around us, a patch of dame's rocket glows like a setting of lavender candles.

At some point, the crescendo peaks, the static slows to a lesser beat, then finally to a patter. The temperature has dropped about ten degrees, but daylight is returning. The warblers shake off the water one last time, fluff their feathers, and fly away. I loosen my drawstrings. An oriole, a thrush, blackbirds, begin to sing. A flicker rattles nearby. Titmice and chickadees patrol the twigs again. The trees seem so very green.

May 24

May spins by so swiftly. It always seems so, but this May really has been shorter; a sliver of March slipped into the middle of it, somehow. Frost has covered lawns and shrubs on at least four mornings in the last week. In the evenings, sheets thrown over the newly planted tomatoes and flowers have lent the neighborhood the aura of Halloween. But yesterday the sun melted all that away, and today a titmouse and a wren are marching me up the hill to find those thrushes. Ahead, a towhee and a catbird call.

The early morning is warm, but rather gray. Rain has been predicted. And if May is slipping away, so too are its apples; few are left, and they're tattered. Ferns and dame's rocket have taken their place.

Bird song fills the air. Orioles, towhees, cardinals, wrens, flickers, song sparrows, and several unidentified others seem to take turns shouting from their various leafy stages. The vireo doesn't take turns. His unrelenting clamor clatters down from somewhere in the upper stories of a nearby elm. It's not unlovely; it just doesn't stop. A rose-breasted grosbeak ghosts through. I'd dearly love to hear him sing, but neither he nor the thrushes do.

In college, the book "The Territorial Imperative" upset me deeply. Its premise was that birdsong isn't singing as we know it: beauty for its own sake. Rather, it's functional and often quite aggressive. Bluebirds, foxes, people… all require home and hunting space, and only those able to take and keep their piece of the earth reproduce. Birdsong is a show of strength. That was troubling. The grosbeak's arias and the thrush's fluting were surely a greater thing than a farmer rushing into the night, shotgun in hand and dog at his side, to run off an intruder. Forty years later, I think better of the farmer and no less of the birds. Now I hear, in birdsong and much else, the joy of living: fierce and lusty and urgent and very much for a purpose—and beautiful.

One of the "unidentified other" bird songs that led me up the hill was decidedly unmusical and, to me, unlovely. It sounded like a mixture of the Three Stooges' "nyuck nyuck nyuck" and someone with a case of very hard and closely spaced hiccups. Unlovely, yes, but also exciting, because I was pretty sure it belonged to a yellow-billed cuckoo. Cuckoos, to me, have always been rather exotic birds: long, lean, furtive shadows slipping half-seen through the canopy. At the moment, though, one is hanging upside down from a thin oak-bough fifty feet above me. It tweezers a caterpillar from a leaf below with its long, curved bill, rights itself with a flutter, and, with its dignity restored, gulps the caterpillar down. So much for exotica.

I think I like the bird even more, now that it's dropped its veil of elusiveness. There's something endearing about the humped shoulder, the curved bill, and that ridiculous song. Besides, what is a birdsong? What's the difference between a "call" and a "song"? Some might say that melody is the key, but the dissonance—to my ears—of 20th century classical music has weakened that argument for me. I suppose that music is in the ear of the beholder and, since female cuckoos find music in sounds that are very like someone choking on a piece of meat, out of deference to differing tastes, I'll call it a song.

The cuckoo is sharing the oak and its caterpillars with a yellow warbler. Neither is singing now; they're far too busy helping the oak with its bug problem. In the strip of meadow that was treated with Roundup—just 90° away, by binoculars—a variety of birds are also gleaning for bugs. The strip is shriveled, crisp and brown, a startling contrast to the rippling greens around it. But the birds don't seem to mind. Tree and barn swallows buzz the brittle stubble. Bluebirds peer down and pounce as they did when it was green. Robins, field and song sparrows, a flicker, and even an oriole stalk the scorched earth; they seem even to prefer it. It looks like this brief interlude of plant death is a nightmare for the insects and heaven for the birds.

Avalanches, fire, Roundup—I never can guess who will suffer and who will thrive when the sword falls.

The wind has grown stronger as I've stood, ruminating. Fully-leafed maples toss their heads like horses ready for the race. Thick curds of cloud float on a thin gray sky. I didn't dress for rain, so it may be time to go. As I lean against the cherry tree, a chickadee skips from branch to branch, nearer and nearer, till he's an arm's length away and looking me in the eye. After a brief inspection, he skips away. I start down the hill.

But now the sun breaks through. There's time to check the pond.

The cattails are knee-high swords of green. Among the lily pads, pairs of goggly eyes bulge out at me. All around, the shore groans with the woes of bullfrog life—though I can't imagine what those woes might be. This seems like bullfrog heaven. Until I look a little closer.

A tree and several large branches have fallen into the pond near the outlet. One of those branches looks rather like the forearm of a giant, lifted languidly from beneath the water, wrist bent, and fingers dangling back into the pond. Five painted turtles have clambered up from the elbow and lay now in line, head to tail, with the largest at the head and the tail of the smallest dragging in the water. They look like five cars, waiting for the light to change. And perhaps the analogy is apt, for three feet ahead of them, entwined upon the branch's wrist, three rather large brown northern water snakes sunbathe. The larger two appear to be 1-2 inches in diameter and 2-3 feet long. A few feet away, on another branch, a two-footer lies stretched out full-length. Rather more alertly than before, I look about for more. A couple of feet from my boot toe, a little guy about a foot long and pencil thick is curled up on a stump, watching me. He and the other four are plain chocolate brown with yellow "chins" and only a hint of yellow lateral markings. But on a willow root a few feet from me, a three-footer with classical field guide markings lies curled and also watching me. He tires of my stares, peers into the water behind the root, then flows like a muddy rivulet into the pond. Without a ripple, the two waters meet, mingle, and are one.

Breathless, on tiptoes, I search for some sign of him—in vain. He has simply disappeared. Surely he's slipped off to some safer place—the middle of the pond, perhaps. That's it: the middle of the pond. But he could be right beneath my feet!

Now I know why the bullfrogs groan.

May 27

Today, I'm trying a new area for my thrush-hunt. On earlier jaunts, I heard wood thrush calls from the other stream that feeds the pond, Grom Run. It's no bigger than the little stream that flows through the Braille Trail; I don't know who or what "Grom" refers to. In any case, it bubbles pleasantly through a mature woodland of oak, walnut, hickory, and tulip trees. I'm walking beside it on Spur Trail, to the tune of a Carolina wren. At one point, the singing becomes annoyed chatter. Perhaps there's a nest nearby.

About a hundred years ago, J. D. Brown built the farmhouse, barn, and outbuildings that now house Latodami. The farm was in operation until 1969 when, as part of the Richard Horning estate, it was put up for sale. The North Area Environmental Council, on learning that the family hoped the farm would remain intact and be used as an educational center, encouraged the County to purchase it as an addition to North Park. This was done, and Joe Grom, a well-known local biology teacher, was hired as the Interpretive Naturalist. Joe developed a series of programs that provided hands-on experience of nature for county residents of all ages and abilities. In 1970, for example, he and the North Hills Jaycees built the Braille Trail to enable the visually handicapped to experience nature, too. His health began to fail in the late 1980's, and in 1987 Meg Scanlon, who had been an intern working with him, assumed the full-time position of Interpretive Naturalist. Since then, she has continued and expanded the programs Joe began. A few years ago, as she and two governmental engineers were looking at a map of the local watershed, they noticed that the stream along Brown Road had no name. Meg suggested that it be named after Joe Grom. I can't think of a better memorial: a woodland stream, with thrushes.

I don't know why seeing a wood thrush is so important to me. Simply hearing one should be enough—no, far more than enough. I like a lot of music; some music, I love; some leaves me with tears rolling down my cheeks and a sob caught in my throat, straining to absorb one note more without bursting. The high registers of Isaac Stern's violin in Brahms' Violin Concerto do that to me. So does almost every note from James Galway's golden flute. If Mr. Galway had feathers, he'd be a wood thrush. It's known as the flautist of the woods. It's song tumbles from the trees in silver splashes. If ears were a cup, you'd find me dashing madly from tree to tree, stretching to catch every drop. The thrush is pretty enough, rather like a robin with a spotted breast. But it's his voice that stops me utterly. So why, when I see him, does my grin broaden even past my ears?

At the moment, several thrushes up and down Grom Run are taking their census. One near me sings his two phrases, the first rising, the second falling into a trill. Answers trickle down from the hillsides. I'm enraptured and grateful. Grateful that wood thrushes seem to be thriving here, for their numbers are falling in the northeast. One problem seems to be that leaching of calcium from the Appalachian soil by acid rain is decimating the woodland invertebrates that the

Grom Run

thrushes live on. Forest fragmentation and the accompanying cowbirds are also a problem here. Deforestation in Central America is taking their winter habitat. I doubt that anyone knows what problems they face on their migration route.

Someone has said that the ephemeral is the most beautiful. Surely, there is sadness at the heart of great beauty, for we ourselves are ephemeral. Perhaps that deepens our appreciation. But I listen to the thrushes all summer, as long as they sing, as long as they stay. And I wait, in eager, impatient anticipation, for their return. Though sadness may sit at the heart of great beauty, its soul is joy.

Along my path, streamside flowers are blooming in profusion: dame's rocket, marsh marigold, bird's-eye primrose, and a few garlic mustard stalks that are just dropping their leaves and going to seed. The skunk cabbage here are huge.

I've since learned that the "bird's-eye primrose" is actually a primula. It's a domestic primrose that has escaped from a lady's garden upstream. So the gorgeous scarlet blossoms that dot the shores and shoals of Grom Run are akin to kudzu and Asian bittersweet: ranks of the horsemen of the Ghengis Khans of the plant world. I'm sure that the lady had no idea she was releasing something that might upset what natural balance is left in the area. I suspect that every time we visit a nursery, we risk adding to the problem.

But will primula overrun Grom Run and escape into western Pennsylvania? Will these lovely flowers displace skunk cabbage or some other valuable native plant? The question of why some alien species become invaders and others don't is a major area of research today. The absence of natural enemies surely helps alien populations explode, but that can't be the whole answer because some imported species thrive and others don't. Recent research has shown that allelopathy—the secretion of chemicals into the soil to inhibit the growth of competitors—is the weapon that Eurasian spotted knapweed is using to invade the west and it's suspected to be the weapon of purple loosestrife, an invader of marshlands in the east. Someday, the local plants will develop resistance to these new poisons, as their European counterparts have done. I doubt that anyone can guess how long that will take, though.

Meanwhile, primula is marching down Grom Run. Meg Scanlon says that, if I lop off those beautiful red heads, it won't propagate. So I will.

The path wanders up the hillside into a grove of ironwoods, tulip trees, elms, and hickories. Early sunshine slants down through the leaves. The canopy is still a little thin here. The nut trees have only the very first tiny leaves. All this new growth must attract a lot of insects and caterpillars; the insectivores have been busy in the treetops all month.

Squirrels like them, too. Right now, a fox squirrel is swaying precariously on the whippy ends of an elm nearby. He clambered back to sturdier footing when I stationed myself by this large pine, but I guess I look harmless, for now he's back on the trapeze.

A wood thrush is singing loudly and still invisibly nearby. And now his cousin, a veery, flutes his eerie melody. He's close and he's—there! On a branch ten yards away at eye level. His song is rather ghostly and certainly unique: he sings harmony with himself! Effortlessly, a music slides out so complex that Pavarotti, Domingo, and Carrerra might match it--but they'd surely turn a bit red. Yet twice a minute he casually tosses his pebble and ripples of Bach flow out to haunt the woodland around him. Before I wish it, he quietly vanishes into the wings.

The avian analog to our larynx is the syrinx. It straddles the point where the two bronchial tubes meet to form the trachea, so two separate air currents flow into it. Its musculature is able to control the two flows independently, so it is able to produce two notes simultaneously.

Five thrush "cousins" breed in Latodami: the wood thrush, hermit thrush, veery, bluebird, and robin.

There are other singers, of course—a yellowthroat among the barberries, a scarlet tanager high in a maple—but their time isn't now. A scratchy one-note rasps through the trees from high up the hill behind me. Perhaps it is time for a great-crested flycatcher, but I can't see him and don't know his call well enough to be sure. He surely flies better than he sings. Red squirrels climb better than they sound, too, but one on the tulip tree a few feet away is about to treat me to his whole larynx. He's trembling with annoyance, first head up, then head down. If I would look his way, he'd let me have it—but I don't. So finally he just scampers around the tree and hence upstairs.

As a nuthatch spirals down a tree some distance away, a yellow flash with dark wings and a black eyebar flits through the leaves. I've never seen a blue-winged warbler, but this might be one. He leaves, and I consult the guidebook. It's a little strange, I suppose: who cares if I'm positive? Is it a big deal? Well, do you count all your golf strokes? So yes, it is a big deal, and I'm not sure. But he'll probably be back. In the meantime, a catbird is pretty entertaining, and chipmunks are scampering about. A trail biker huffs up the trail, head down and pumping. I'm only a few feet off the path, but he doesn't see me.

And now there's the flash of yellow again, but this time, he's closer and busy with his hunting. He moves quickly, from twig to twig, in and out of the leaves, but the black eye-line is distinct, the wings are blue-gray with faint wing-bars, and his head is all yellow. So the blue-winged warbler has just joined my life list! (It isn't a hole-in-one, but it certainly is a birdie.)

Down the hill, now. Along the stream, two Carolina wrens are whirring and rattling around a chipmunk that's poking about in the underbrush near where I'd thought a nest might be. I'm afraid that he's found it, and that I'm about to bow to another of the little tragedies you witness if you look at nature too closely. But though he's getting a lot of attention from the wrens, he isn't paying much attention to them, and disappears up the hill. The wrens begin to hunt among the grasses and twigs with a vigor that speaks against tragedy. One carries a limp caterpillar into the dark center of a bush, where I now see a third wren. There are more in there. I count three chicks scattered about in the bush, preening and chirping, as the parents dash about, hunting and feeding, in a churring flurry.

More limp caterpillars plunge down dark chirping maws while I look on, smiling broadly. Odd, how one meal seems like a tragedy and another doesn't.

May 30

Some citizens of the woods are natural clowns: chipmunks, squirrels, and jays, particularly. But not today. Today, I'm standing in the middle of a chase that is deadly serious.

I'm at the base of a black cherry tree that stands twenty or thirty yards from the mass of vines and branches that may hide a blue jay's nest. Until a minute ago, I stood surrounded by peacefulness: green leaves, pendant white flowers of the cherry, and the tootling, twittering springtime symphony. Suddenly, the bark above me rattled and bits fell on my hat and shoulders. I looked up sharply— directly into the eyes of a red squirrel that was coming down fast. It turned ninety degrees without slowing and spiraled back up the trunk with two jays right behind. Now I'm in the eye of a hurricane of chase and evasion. The squirrel has gone back up the cherry, across to another tree in a long leap, down into a maze of grapevines, zigzagging, backtracking, always spiraling, even on the thinnest branches, and always at flat-out speed. It doesn't chatter, it doesn't scold—it just flees through the trees as though its life depends on it. It probably does. The jays are utterly silent, too, and only inches behind in cold, quiet, deadly pursuit. The squirrel's hope is unpredictability, its flight utterly random. Up, down, and across the trees they fly. I've never seen greater athleticism; never seen higher stakes. After minutes, maybe hours—I have no idea—they disappear. A zag in the chase takes them into trees beyond my range.

Moments later, a jay returns from that direction and quietly checks the grapevine tangle. I don't know what became of the squirrel. It probably escaped. But I'm not inclined to look in the grapevines for the nest. A hairy woodpecker happens by and, though he's the jay's size and has a long wicked bill, the jay chases him away, too. A third jay appears and, in a flurry of furious blue, leaves.

A titmouse has been calling from the treetops all around, but the jays haven't made a sound.

Would a red squirrel raid a blue jay nest? Yes. Would the jays injure or kill the squirrel? I don't know. Jays do raid the nests of other birds and have been reported to kill and eat smaller birds at feeders, so they probably could. But I doubt that they would have to. I think that competition in the wild is so intense that being slowed by even a minor injury could, ultimately, be fatal. So predators seldom risk injury for a meal. Was the squirrel in real danger? He probably didn't know, assumed the worst, and ran like hell.

The windmill in the upper meadow seems like a focus for crossing birds, like an island in the sea. I've left the woods, and now a towhee has just flown by my head. Song sparrows are gleaning in the grapevines; a wren sings among the leaves. A tree swallow is making frequent stops at one of the bird boxes. S/he perches at the hole, peers in for a moment, then curls away into the hunt. I haven't seen it remove any fecal sacs.

The feces of the chicks of many species of birds are surrounded by a membrane to form a "fecal sac". When chicks are in the nest, the parents can often be seen carrying these small white bags in their bills for deposit somewhere inconspicuous.

The current king of the large sycamore tree in the middle of the meadow is a male red-winged blackbird. He has just chased two other males out of it, and now is in reckless pursuit of a passing crow. This is the season of unhesitating heroism. The wrens, the jays, the blackbird, most parents I know—all understand one another.

We understand a mother's fearlessness—that's obvious—but we also pick up not-so-obvious "minor" changes in behavior. A doe dressed in her beautiful reddish-brown springtime coat strides across the meadow a little west of me. She doesn't linger, but seems in no particular hurry. Something about her casualness in the meadow at midmorning feels odd. Perhaps she just checked on a fawn hidden in the grass. If so, she won't go far. She disappears into the woods, and I exhale. She didn't see me. For those few moments, I'd forgotten the myriad of man-eating midges that swarm around my head. If it weren't for the Off, they'd surely be On. I squash one. That funny "looked-at" feeling prickles at my neck, so I turn toward the woods. The doe is just inside the tree line with her ears up and her eyes on me. She huffs at me. I turn away, more certain that a fawn is curled up in the grass not far away.

Or maybe not. A second deer appears in the meadow, but he moves and acts more like a buck. He trots right at my little island, then stops. Ears up, he peers into my grove, careful to keep a screen of leaves between us. He dithers, turns, takes a step one way, then the other. He's north of me. There must be a very light south wind. And Off must work on deer, too. He decides, and in just three or four utterly majestic white-flagged leaps, he's into the woods and gone.

The birds aren't so shy. Moreover, this little oasis in the meadow appears to be common ground. In spite of all their territoriality, all kinds of birds have passed through without contest: towhees, robins, blackbirds, goldfinches, cardinals, and song sparrows, to name a few. In the background, I've been hearing what seem to be a brown thrasher's couplets. Now, as I'm about to leave, the silhouette of a thrasher sits on a bluebird box across the meadow.

So, I walk past that bird box on my way out. A pair of thrashers are perched at the edge of the woods, and fly into the meadow grass ahead of me. They don't reappear, but a Baltimore oriole does, and a man walks by with his dog ranging beside him and a large coffee cup in his hand.

As I walk down the hill, sunshine falls on an indigo bunting in a flowering black cherry tree across the clearing. His iridescent blueness, the tree as green and white background, all ablaze in the golden morning sunshine—I'm reminded again of Van Gogh, trying to capture such colors. I'd love to, too, with words. But I found, as a small boy, that fireflies don't fit in a bottle. Oh the bugs do, of course. It's the magic that doesn't. So, too, with buntings and flowering trees. Come outside and see them.

June

Dogwood Blossoms

Just half a moon ago
the dogwoods gleamed in the cool light
like woodland brides in snowy lace,
glowing soft and heart-break lovely
midst the forest's silhouettes, awaiting
dark wild princes of the night.

But dreams so shimmering can't last.
Now their nuptial dance is done,
the moon is dark, their petals—
velvet once—now crisp
and strewn like turnings
beneath the lathe of Spring.

As I caress the crinkled hems
of cast-off veils and gowns,
my gaze drifts sadly down
the long, uncertain path
that must be trod before
I'll see them dance again.

June 4

The woods and stream along Spur Trail seem rich in wildlife, so I'm here again, though a little late. The thrushes have drawn me back; they must be nesting nearby. The air is full of thrush melodies, but this is a chorus incorporeal. As I walk the muddy streamside trail, one would think the very leaves are singing: music everywhere, no birds.

The plants, at least, stay put. The cast is changing, though. May has gone, and the May apples are bedraggled and mottled with yellow spots. The garlic mustard has shed its flowers and most of its leaves; the stems and seed pods look a bit like green candelabras for some midnight fairy dance. The ferns' time has come. There are once-, twice-, and thrice-cut species in patches and clumps among the rocks and moss-covered corpses of ancient trees. The once-cut variety is Christmas fern, the thrice-cut are woodferns, but I can't name the twice-cut species—yet.

At my stand by an old tulip tree, the veery sings occasionally. He's in the upper stories today. I follow his voice from tree to tree, but can't see him or the other, rather raucous fellow in the same vicinity. But a flycatcher is hunting low in the trees. He's small, with wing bars and eye-ring, so he's probably in the genus Empidonax. Even the experts say that visual identification of the species in that genus is difficult; they often rely on the birds' calls. This one sounds like the recording of the Acadian flycatcher: "wee-chup" with the second syllable cut off abruptly. He's too busy eating the bugs that are trying to eat me to worry about what I'm up to. I'm up to nothing more than cheering him on.

Nearby, a hairy woodpecker tears an old snag apart. A red-bellied woodpecker flies through purposefully. The song of a hooded warbler floats over. At some signal I'm not privy to, the titmice take their census. There were no titmouse calls, now the woods rings with their clear, sharp whistles, loudest right above my head, less loud, then faint and fainter in concentric circles all around me. I wonder how many miles of titmice are in this census. Does it carry all the way to Ohio? They count for several minutes, then stop, for no reason that I can fathom.

The veery appears! He sings that haunting melody, then tumbles into the complex set of squawks that I'd attributed to some "raucous fellow" in the veery's vicinity. It was him! The field guide recordings don't give him credit for the range of noise he's capable of. These calls aren't pretty, but they are complex, and attest to a talented syrinx. Well, what's wrong with playing "Turkey in the Straw" on a Stradivarius?

On my way back down Spur Trail, a doe leaps from a thicket as I pass, but doesn't flee with her tail high. Rather, when I pause by the thicket, she stands watching me over her shoulder. Perhaps a fawn lays trembling a few feet from me? Perhaps, so I walk primly by. The doe runs on ahead, but soon she stops to look back again. I'm reminded of the tales of killdeer that feign a broken wing to draw a predator from their chicks. Now off she goes again. I catch up with her again. I'll bet she'd carry my keys for me if I told her where my car is parked.

She leaves me at the road. But beside the road, a black swallowtail butterfly laps water from the mud. There's contrast: the blue-black velvet wings with a line of pale yellow dots and an orange spot are a vision of fragility and beauty: the mud is…well, mud.

In the pond, a green heron stalks the edge of the cattails. One more reason for the bullfrogs to groan.

June 10

High in a black cherry tree at the edge of the upper meadow, a female Baltimore oriole is hanging upside down from the vanishing point of a whip-thin bough, nibbling the dangling pale-green buttons. *(They're no longer blossoms, nor yet cherries, so what are they called??)* The male sings nonchalantly from a branch that's higher still, but sturdier. He doesn't seem the least bit concerned for her. That's reasonable. She carries her own net. For birds, falling must be fun.

A doe steps into the corner of my eye. I'm in the very middle of both of hers. She had been walking casually from the meadow into the woods, but she seems not to like the looks of me. I watch the orioles and pretend to be a stump. It's amazing how slowly deer move when they doubt your truthfulness, but how quickly when they're sure you lie. She isn't sure. She stares for the longest time—a real stump would be visibly rotting away by now—walks two or three steps as if she were testing thin ice, stops to stare some more. A few more steps and she's into the woods, partly screened by leaves. She looks away, but her ears are aimed at me. At last, she seems satisfied and walks casually down the hill. But satisfied, she is not, nor has she heard about curiosity and the cat. She turns, walks back up the hill until she stands about ten yards away, broadside and staring. I'm a pretty good stump. Now she walks back down the hill to stand, about forty yards away, stamping a foot and huffing. Finally, she melts into the bushes, utterly annoyed. I'm delighted, of course.

All this time, the woods have been busy with birds. Jays, robins, wrens, song sparrows, titmice, and red-winged blackbirds have passed through. Just now, a towhee zips through, low and fast. A vireo, probably the red-eyed species from the incessant, boring song he sings, is somewhere in the canopy. Rather than get as frustrated as the doe, I decide not to look for him.

Instead, the windmill calls from the meadow. Milkweed, thistles, and some small bushes are sprouting in the brown area beside it. That dead zone begins to look like it's reverting to its pre-Roundup state, except for long parallel grooves that score its whole length. The Jolly Green Giant might rake the land like that, but it's more likely the reseeding, done with a planter that doesn't require plowed earth.

To the birds, though, it's still a prime hunting ground. A female bluebird flushes ahead of me. A bird that looks like a thrush flies from the bald brown earth into the bushes around the windmill tower. A thrush out in the open? Maybe it's a thrasher.

But as I settle against the old apple tree, a thrush is rustling about among the bushes. It flies back into the brown area and begins to hunt as if it were a robin. It's a hermit thrush, maybe the very one that eluded me in April. It's acting like a robin, though, and a robin takes offence. After a brief, tornado-like disagreement, the robin, though larger, leaves. The thrush stands just yards away, pumping adrenaline and proud. Reminds me a bit of a victorious professional wrestler.

A female oriole flies away from the sycamore tree. That's odd. Retracing her path leads my eyes to—the nest! It hangs like a rattan purse from the lower branches. Soon the male arrives, peers into the nest, and pokes his head deep into the middle of it. As his head disappears, his tail tips up as a bright yellow flash. Back up he pops, looks all around, and flies away as if nothing has happened. Soon though, the female arrives, to flash just as yellow as he.

The king of that tree—the red-winged blackbird—still sings from the tree's highest bough, but he doesn't seem to mind the constant coming and going of orioles. Indeed, he seems quite lax: a whole flock of blackbirds pass through without any challenge. Some kind of flycatcher hunts from a dead branch. It's too far away for my binoculars and irrelevant to the king.

All is not peace and goodwill, however. A mockingbird lands on the windmill's peak, and all vocal hell breaks loose. If some seabirds portend high seas and storm, the mockingbird portends—indeed, creates—high seas of sound and auditory storm. He seems like the lord of the tower, but he has his Cromwell. A second male appears. The two whirl around the tower, in and out of the leaves, a silent, half-seen cyclone of anger. At last they rest, glaring from their perches and shrieking at each other like rusty hinges on the screen doors of the long-departed farmhouse. One leaves for the top of the sycamore. The other perches on a birdhouse nearby. They look alike to me, so I don't know whether the monarchy has been preserved or not. The queen doubtlessly does.

Mockingbirds seem to be "essentially monogamous," according to Sibley.

Several male goldfinches filter like sunlight through the bushes beneath the sycamore. Underneath the birdhouse, a female flicker drills her own holes in the brown land. Several mourning doves serenely peck at its edge. It appears that the rest of the world doesn't give a fig about the mockingbird wars. I move on, too.

Beside the path that leads down the hill, a dragonfly with black marks on its wings is perched lengthwise on a dead multiflora rose branch near the barn. She appears to be a common whitetail, though she's a hundred yards from the pond. The field guide places the whitetails near slow-moving water. I don't know whether this distance is "near enough" to a dragonfly or not.

This morning has reinforced my belief that May and June are the best months for bird watching: after the migrants have arrived, before the foliage has become so dense the birds are hard to see, and while they're raising families. I feel that I've seen a volume, with white-tailed creatures as bookends.

June 13

Seventeen-year cicadas seemed likely to be the subject today. Woodlands just a few miles west and north of here are humming, as with the continual high-pitched whine of tires on a highway just beyond the trees. But this hum has an eerie pitch, and there is no highway. The sound is coming from bugs.

They haven't come here, though. Not yet, at least. The woods along Spur Trail are quiet, except for birdsong and the tinkling of the stream as it tumbles over pebbles. The veery and a hooded warbler are singing among the trees higher up the hill, so I climb to the base of a huge old tulip tree to watch and listen.

Here, a softer sound, a scratching and rattling, mingles with the warbler's "wee-tee-o." I peek around the tree to find, scuffling among some fallen branches under a large pine a few yards away, a squirming pile of one, two...yes, three fuzzy young raccoons. Legs wave, a ringed tail sticks up, a bandit's face pops out for air and leverage, then plunges back into the melee. As in any scrum of puppies, it's easy to see the parts nipping, chewing, and mauling each other, but not so easy to count individuals. There's one on its back with its legs waving in the air. And there's the tail of an adult disappearing into the ferns and barberry bushes.

The veery is now quite close, and a vireo begins to sing just above my head. I draw back behind the tree to watch them.

After a while, I peek around my tree again. Mama coon is back. She sees me, or movement, at least, and sends the kids shinnying up the tree. She follows, but doesn't seem hurried. She settles among the first branches and peers out.

Rather than keeping them treed for no good reason, I decide to move on. But as I step into the open, a frighteningly savage snarl shatters the woodland silence. Roar after roar rolls down the hillside. It must be her, but it seems too loud, too vicious, for such a small animal. Besides, I'd thought that she'd seen me already. Perhaps something larger was stalking her? Wisdom says to sort this out from somewhere else, so I walk back down to the stream. The snarling stops.

I watch the empty path behind me, breathe deeply to settle my adrenaline. No red-eyed grizzly crashes through the underbrush, hungrily dripping from the jowls. No T-Rex. Nothing. Caught between relief and embarrassment, I can only tip my hat to Mama Coon. Motherhood wins again.

The woods reawakens. The veery, and now a flicker call from nearby. Little ripples tinkle in the stream. A robin lands on a rock, hops into a pool, and takes a loud, splashy bath. It seems loud, now, anyway. A wood thrush flits across the opening to disappear into the bushes. A towhee calls from uphill, and soon follows the thrush into the greenery. A chipmunk scampers down a tree and across the stream on a log.

As the hoot of the 6:00 train fades, with time, into an unnoticed thread in the tapestry of background sound, so some movements weave almost unseen into the warp and the woof of the everyday scene: the scampering of squirrels, the unhurried passages of birds, the flow of the brook. But some movements startle the eye. One just did. Some small brown mammal just slipped across the stream and into the barberries, as sudden and swift as lightning, as smooth and purposeful as a snake. No chipmunk ever moved like that. And now, moments later, a Carolina wren explodes from those same bushes in a cascade of rattling anger. It flutters noisily above the bushes for several minutes, moving always farther from where it erupted. At last, it slips quietly back into the barberry patch from a different direction. I can only guess that a weasel just passed through. For elusiveness, weasels are like foxes, but more so.

I'm standing among knee-high, twice-cut ferns that taper to the base. There don't seem to be any fruit-dots. New York ferns?

It's time to go home, but first, I have to check on the raccoon family. So back up the hill, or rather, halfway up the hill. The binoculars show a long ringed tail dangling from the pine, and then, up the tail, mom, dozing on the broad branch with the kids on her back. She looks like she's sleeping, but I don't see how she could be. The kids are supposed to be napping, but they're not.

June 19

Sunshine is the artist on this golden post-rain morning. It slides up and down gossamer threads as they sway in the gentle breezes. Thin shafts pierce the woods' high canopy, to be caught in the rising mists. Little bugs glow in an instant of fame as they flutter through beams from the windows of heaven. In the meadow, the grasses are bowed and silver with dew till the sun lifts over the trees. Then fire opals flash from their stems.

The meadow could be in the Louvre, to be sure, but it's also breakfast time out there. A small head, dark green above, white below, pokes out of a nearby birdhouse. Its tree swallow parents swoop in, stuff an insect into its wide open mouth, and arc away. The movement is smooth, pure artistry. But unless that chick is an only child, behind the art is a shoving match as the chicks vie for the window seat. On the ground in the brown area, a young thrush tags behind its mother as she hunts. She rushes, head down, to catch a caterpillar, turns to stuff it dangling down the wide young mouth, then stalks the bare earth once again. Others hunt there: a pair of bluebirds, a robin, a chipping sparrow, a mockingbird, but they seem to be hunting for themselves. Their time for self-denial will come soon, I suppose.

The oriole nest still hangs from the sycamore tree, but there isn't any activity around it. Jays, starlings, and the unidentified flycatcher perch all around it, but I see no orioles. So theirs is another partly-told tale.

Still, I can hope that their story is unfolding like that of the wren family at the edge of the meadow. At least three chicks sit among the grapevines, bemused balls of fluff with needles for beaks, waiting to be fed. Every few minutes, a parent appears, stuffs something down a throat, and disappears. The chicks flutter from perch to perch. They're pretty good fliers already, and would be hard to catch, so the oh so vulnerable time has passed. But, so far, they have nowhere better to go.

The high whine of cicadas calls me down the hill. Along that path, the dame's rocket have stripped off flowers and leaves to disappear into skeletal stalks of seeds. Now is the time for yarrow, teasel, and, farther down, marsh marigold. A dark green damselfly hunts from a broad leaf, much in the style of the feathered flycatchers. But the cicadas elude me. They must be pretty far away.

That's just as well. I've seen them and the damage they do on a golf course and the surrounding woods west of here. The insects themselves looked much like our annual cicadas, except that these had orange eyes and a red stripe along their sides from thorax to abdomen. Their flight was also like that of the annual cicadas: slow, blundering and reminiscent of bumblebees. Nor were their numbers so very exceptional. I had expected clouds of them and trees stripped entirely of leaves. I guess I had expected a locust plague of Biblical proportions. Instead, golfers who paid more attention to the game may not have noticed them at all. But my game lends itself to investigations of the rough, and there I found cicadas in lines on the branches of the hardwood saplings. They seemed to be waiting to move up the branch, but I suppose they were laying eggs, with each clutch a cicada-length apart. I didn't see any on the spruces or pines, so apparently they're selective. On the fairway, cicada bodies were scattered about, rather like Japanese beetles after a spraying. I don't know whether this reflects their normal life cycle or the toxicity of golf courses. Their normal life cycle does include laying eggs in the terminal twigs of trees, and that did appear to be pretty damaging. The oaks, especially, and other hardwoods in the area seemed to be festooned with brown tinsel, as though in some Grinch-inspired parody of Christmas. It was, rather, the death of this year's growth. But the ages of most of the trees are several times seventeen, so the damage must be temporary.

Seventeen years underground seems a high price to pay for a few days of clumsy flight, especially when it ends in futility on the hostile grass of a golf course. That's blatant anthropomorphism, of course. And I fear that my fantasies were no kinder than the greens-keeper's poisons. I had hoped to see flocks of exotic birds—gulls from the Great Salt Lake, perhaps, or cuckoos (both black- and yellow-billed)—feasting on clouds of buzzing cicadas. One cuckoo did slip half-seen through the trees as I searched for an errant golf ball. But there were no flocks, no clouds.

The taboo against anthropomorphism is one I cheerfully disregard. Like miscegenation and heterodoxy, anthropomorphism is a perfectly natural impulse, and the exhortations against all three are lines drawn across a continuum, usually, I think, to enable one group to do the unthinkable to another. How can we enslave others if they aren't somehow inferior, or consign innocents to eternal damnation? How can we have souls and do as we like to the rest of creation if humans aren't fundamentally superior? Such divisions make us feel better about ourselves, I suppose, and surely simplify a bewilderingly complex reality–but at a cost. Think of what we do to each other in the names of our orthodoxies.

But apes can use sign language meaningfully, pets exhibit jealousy and joy, birds use tools, the mourning of elephants looks very like the mourning of people. The more I look around, the more I find that the lines that separate seem artificial, similarities and interdependence, real. That raccoon's rage makes sense to me: I've felt parental worry and protectiveness, too. If that's instinct, well, it's moving both of us similarly. I can write about it, while she can't, but that's a difference in degree, not kind. She's learned the frailties and rewards of the local garbage cans, and that's more practical to her than a word processor. We understand one another remarkably well: she was as aggressive as, but not more than, she needed to be. I may respond in kind if she doesn't stay out of the garbage. Still, I believe, more and more, that she, I, and the myriad of others are, if not equals, at least partners in the same grand undertaking.

June 26

A snapping turtle is waddling across the Latodami driveway as I arrive this morning. Her journey from the pond up the hill looks like an egg-laying pilgrimage. I'm tempted to park right here so I can watch, but that might be too intrusive. So I park in the proper area and, by the time I've returned, she's disappeared.

Apparently, she would have ignored me if I had followed her. I missed an opportunity.

The canopy above Grom Run is thick, green, and complete now. Bird's call from among the leaves—I can identify the veery, wood thrush, red-bellied woodpecker, Carolina wren, red-eyed vireo, and hooded warbler, and there are surely more—but they're all quite invisible up there. The woodland sings with disembodied voices.

There is more to see around my feet. A fox squirrel cautiously climbs down a tree to the little stream for a drink. Nearby, the dame's rocket are nearly gone, and in their place, jewelweed and a patch of tall plants with nettle-like leaves and strangely shaped scarlet flowers is growing. The field guide suggests bee-balm. While I muse upon the flora, some fauna rustles behind me. A red squirrel glares at me from a tree trunk a couple of arm-lengths away. It scampers back up a few feet, back down, now around the tree to peer from behind the trunk, up the tree, back down. I'm probably in its way, but it doesn't scold me. It just doesn't seem to know what to do about me. Finally, it goes up and over. And, having complicated the squirrel's life enough, I hike across the road and up the hill to the upper meadow.

The hill is steep. This puts patches of ferns at eye level as I climb slowly upward. So I gasp to the overhanging pines that this is a great opportunity to identify another kind of fern. These ferns are small, not tapered, thrice-cut, with fragile green stems. My first guess (guide book in hand) is oak fern. But the fruitdots suggest bracken. Steep hills are good teachers of humility. I'm out of shape and even more aware of how little I know of the world around me.

Two hundred feet higher, at the interface of young woodland and meadow, the cast of birds is different and more visible: flickers, blackbirds, towhees, and tree swallows, to name just a few. The wren family is in the same area as last week, but now I only see three. One, surely a juvenile, is loudly chasing a second from branch to branch, and seems to be begging. Perhaps its siblings have learned self-sufficiency, this is the whiner, and mom has decided that, like it or not, today is graduation.

There are ferns here, too, but these are so unfernlike that they must be sensitive ferns. Two bird songs from the treetops baffle me, but at least I'm pretty sure of the ferns.

July

Drought

Today, again, the sun glared down
on a cracked and dusty land,
on tortured leaves, crisp and curled,
on memories of streams, now twisted paths
of clattering stone.

Tonight, though,
hope bulges up against the stars,
rumbles portentously,
billows with promises.

Breezes whisper sweet release,
grow to gusts that murmur
to the swaying trees of Earth Mother,
wound about with sheets of rain
and flash of diamond in her hair,
marching on the gasping hills. And now

She comes:
Queen of Thunder looming over us,
her tiny desiccated supplicants.
We laugh; hold out our hats...

but she is empty:
dry lightning, and retreat.
She gathers up her skirts,
steps over us, and gazing eastward,
thunders promises that dwindle
into grumbles in the hollow night.

Flickering with fire,
silhouettes of rain mountains
drift away beyond recall.
Sharp stars glitter once again.
We pace the brittle grass,
hot, restless and annoyed.

July 1

The waning moon, half-gone, hangs above the pond mists. The sun hasn't risen, but the birds have. The songs of towhees, robins, Carolina wrens, house wrens, and red-winged blackbirds drip from the trees. Barn swallows chitter as they swoop above the pond. Water rattles loudly down the overflow drain. The pond itself is now half-covered with lily pads. That means that half is only five feet deep or less. The other half is thick with several kinds of water grasses. I'm told that, in ten years or so, the pond will be a marsh. It seems like it's nearly there today.

North Park Lake, which lies downstream, has been heavily silted by the development all around the park. Latodami's feeder streams, though, originate in and flow through undisturbed woodland. Much of the silt in the pond washed down Grom Run from a catastrophic rupture of the water storage tower up the hill. But the current eutrophication seems to be natural, with maybe some help from "nutrients" from the houses above the barn.

With a harsh squawk, a green heron alights high in the bony branches of a dead elm. It seems to be on the verge of soaring down to the shallows to hunt, but hesitates, then flops from branch to branch, as if in watchful indecision. I'm probably the problem. At last, with another squawk, it flaps away.

Two days later, Meg Scanlon showed me the heron's nest. It was just a loose mat of twigs laid in a hawthorn tree across the road from the pond. It was very much like the nests that I saw higher up the hill in January. Green herons are less than half as tall as blue herons and a lot lighter, so their nests are proportionally smaller—maybe a foot in diameter.

The chicks had apparently fledged; the nest was empty and few droppings remained in the grasses below. I didn't see younger herons with the adult in the elm, but I wonder if she was looking for a safe place to hunt with them. A green heron often stalks along logs that project into a pond, its long neck drawn back very much like an arrow on a bowstring. As the prey draws closer, it tends to flick its tail, nervously, I suppose. I'm reminded of my cats.

A tree-sized serviceberry bush leans over the pond near the dead elm. A robin and a veery hang from the branch tips, snapping up the hanging green berries. It seems a bit odd, since the birds are a bit large for such acrobatics and these aren't ripe berries—I think ripe serviceberries are black. But green serviceberries must really be good. A red-bellied woodpecker arrives, wings hugely wide as it brakes among the tiny high branches, to swing wildly on them as it lunges greedily for the little green balls. The fat man who bathed with the ducks in October is on a trapeze with the robins in July.

Others display more dignity. A phoebe has perched, erect and alert, on bare branches all around the pond. Occasionally, it loops out and back, gracefully and quite under control. A female blackbird casually walks the slender boughs of a willow, in subdued striped brown loveliness against the light green background.

I've also been watching the bullfrogs. One in the middle of the pond must be sitting on submerged grass; it appears to be sitting on its reflection, creating a striking double image. After a while, though, even such artistry pales: bullfrogs don't move much. Bullfrog-watching must be the epitome of sedentary sports.

So, I'm startled when something does move. A muskrat emerges at my feet to nibble some cattails on the bank. As it passes me, it also passes within a foot of a bullfrog. Were I to move, that frog would leap shrieking for deeper water, but it doesn't budge as the muskrat passes. Dumb animals? These seem to know what they need to know. The muskrat slips back into the pond, to reappear among the lily pads. It seems to be nibbling on them as it swims through. Quietly, casually, it slips across the pond, under and through its edible world, finally to dive and disappear on the other side.

July 9

I'm accustomed to being king of the woods. Oh, in Alaska I deferred to the moose and grizzlies, of course. But I've walked woodlands from Minnesota to Pennsylvania with impunity. The critters may ignore, avoid, or flee from me, but they've never chased me. Well, there was the mother raccoon last month and a rattlesnake on the Kalamazoo River in Michigan, but they didn't chase me—they just encouraged me to leave.

This morning, a large buck with antlers in velvet is challenging those rules. As I walked up the hill toward the upper meadow, he stood motionless at the other side of a small grassy area. He should have leaped away, snorting, with his white tail waving. I would have been sorry to have scared him so unnecessarily, but that's the way it goes. But he didn't leap away. He wasn't frightened. He just stood there, staring at me.

After a while, I turned back up the hill to go about my business. Now, a couple of hundred yards up the hill, I have just looked back over my shoulder to find— the buck, following me! An acquaintance was once chased out of a clearing by a buck in rut, but that was in November. What's on this guy's mind? Actually, he isn't acting aggressively: no snorting or stomping, no antler waving or agitation. But he is following me. We stand for minutes, sizing each other up from across the clearing. I see a creature my size, unbowed and better armed. I don't know what he sees. My growing annoyance, perhaps. Hands on my hips, I speak sternly to him, as though he were a bad dog. He doesn't even blink. So I pull the pruning saw from my fanny pack, open it slowly, and tap the flat blade against my knee. I remind myself of the rattlesnake: tap, tap, tap—coiled and glaring at the intruder. He still seems unmoved. Minutes pass. Finally, he lowers his head, flicks his tail, and grudgingly, unhurriedly, disappears into the trees.

I take a deep breath, turn, and walk to the meadow. On the path behind me, I see—nothing. That's good. On the path ahead, a young rabbit bounds away. Its white tail is doing what it should. This is better.

The woods and meadow seem quieter and emptier than they did in June. The usual birds are singing. A pair of bluebirds is hunting the meadow below from the boughs of a locust. A nuthatch works up the tree trunk. Swallows sweep the airs above the grasses. But the pace of bird life isn't as frantic, the bird songs aren't piled on top of each other, as in May and June. A robin will sing for a while, then silence. A cardinal will begin. They almost take turns. The mood seems much more relaxed.

The meadow is different, too. The unmowed, mostly alien grasses have gone to seed. Their tawny heads bow in waves before the light west winds. The "brown strip" that was poisoned and replanted, on the other hand, is now a dark, healthy-looking green.

And as I walk the deer paths through the woods, I sense a change in me, too. My pace is usually slow, my intent to be as quiet and aware as possible. But today, my caution is less theoretical, a bit more Alaskan. The buck has taught me a little humility.

Just before I leave the woods, a spotted fawn bursts from a patch of high grass and leaps away, white flag flying. It probably should have stayed where it was well hidden. My first thought is to wonder if the doe is nearby. Then I wonder if the buck is its father.

July 17

After several weeks without rain, Grom Run has lost its voice. It has gone beyond a dry hoarseness into desiccated silence. It no longer leaps over the rocks along its path. Indeed, it has been reduced to a thread strung thinly among them. An occasional fluttering of silver among the brown stones is the only sign of a faint pulse. The larger pools are now thin, flat puddles, wrinkled only by the little circles of trapped water striders. As I walk the streambed, my footsteps clatter—the voices of dry rocks rubbing together.

I'm saddened, but perhaps overly. So far, this is just a dry spell, not a drought. Even though most of the streambed is only damp mud now, life is certainly going on, even there. I've just turned over about a dozen stones and, beneath two, found little brown salamanders. They're about two inches long and have a stripe down their backs, so I think they are northern dusky salamanders.

A patch of bee-balm grows beside the Run, and it's in full bloom. The flowers remind me of a rooster's head: bright red comb above, wattle below, and the mouth between. An odd shape for a flower, but a ruby-throated hummingbird likes it. He/she lands on a dead twig above me, decides that the oaf standing stupidly in the middle of breakfast is harmless, and drops down into the same pasture that a bumblebee is grazing in. The bumblebee hangs heavily from the flower's lower lip. The plant bows as he hauls himself up until his whole head is buried in the flower's mouth. He guzzles, then drops free and rumbles off to find another. The bee-balm leaps back to vertical. I think I can hear its sigh of relief. In comparison, the hummingbird's approach is surgical. It hovers in front of the flower, inserts its long hypodermic needle, withdraws its mouthful, backs away, darts to the next patient, and so it methodically visits the whole ward. Since pollination is the flower's goal, the bumblebee's clumsy pollen-smeared hug is probably better for the flower than the hummingbird's clinical visit, but it certainly doesn't look like it ought to be.

Now up the path into the woods that overlooks the stream. The woods ring with the voices of vireos, towhees, a wood thrush, titmice, robins, a nuthatch, a flicker, and the red-bellied woodpecker—I fear this is becoming a litany—that I hear but can't see in the canopy.

But as the morning sun filters through that canopy, its very obliqueness sometimes reveals subtleties I'd otherwise miss. So it is today. Among the backlit tulip leaves, a horizontal ray touches a fragile web. Faint, hardly to be seen, it pulsates like a jellyfish in breezes so slight that the leaves don't even tremble. But this fragile beauty of the moment bows to a vaster physics: the earth creaks around another fraction of a degree and the web disappears.

The angle of the sun takes one vision away, but presents a new one. Just below where the web was, a tiny spinning silver circle appears. It seems to be a wheel that is whirling, unsupported, in space. I guess, though, that it's a bug trying to escape from a strand dangling from the web. I pass my finger above it. The circle collapses into a mote that sparkles for a moment in the sun as it flies away.

As usual, as I stand quietly, the bird songs begin to grow bodies. A wren and a veery hunt among the grapevines on a tulip tree. The veery looks a little decrepit, as if it has begun to molt—the first stage of the autumn migration. Feathers get battered during the spring migration and the rigors of mating and raising a family. This is the veery's new set for the flight to the neotropics. A brown and yellow warbler seems to be eating the small green berries of the spicebushes along the path. I'm pretty sure she's a female hooded or Wilson's warbler. Two phoebes flit about down by the streambed. One seems to be waiting for the other, so it's probably another parent feeding a nearly-grown fledgling. Back among the grapevines, an oriole is eating the green grapes. I begin to wonder if many berries ever get to ripen.

The sun is higher yet, now, and draws me again to a tinier world. A little red spider is climbing an invisible ladder into the leaves. When it reaches my height, it rests, swaying in the breeze. It could gaze directly into my eyes. Perhaps it does. Then up it goes, into the leaves, hand over hand over hand...

Without the spider's ascent, I would never have seen them. Luckily, my eyes' trajectory overruns the web and, far higher, in a beam of golden light among the tulip leaves, is caught by a flickering of tiny dancing insects. It might have been a squadron of WWI biplanes, hovering and darting in a combat long ago and far away, for the thin black bodies and wide translucent wings have more the appearance of distant aeroplanes than of little bugs much closer. Indeed, their flight is combative, reminiscent of the darting and chasing of dragonflies in miniature, rather than of the looping mating flights of midges. And as they hover, shimmering among the high sunbeams, as my eyes adjust to the world of the microscopic, I realize that they swim in a rain of twinkling golden specks, motes tinier even than they. Pollen from the tulip trees, I suppose. Or fairy dust. Who knows? Though I wade through this deluge of tittles, I feel buoyant, somehow. If this rainfall continues, I may become so drenched by it that I, too, float among the sunbeams and tulip leaves.

Larger movement breaks my trance. A pair of tanagers rows more heavily through the treetops. A loose feather flops from her wing, which makes me wonder if their molt has begun. But he is still clothed in dazzling scarlet, so I guess not. After the molt, the field guides say, he'll wear her more modest yellow and brown. But I doubt that I'll recognize him.

As I walk the path toward my car, a jay is chased from tree to tree by a fluffier, even louder, version of itself. It has to be another parent weaning a reluctant fledging. But in the case of the jay, I'm not so sympathetic. Adult jays deserve their teenagers.

August

Cobwebs

Look sunward and you'll see them:
slender cables stretching
twig to twig, tree to tree,
shimmering deadly little rainbows
to snare the lace-winged dancers
as they court among the beams.

Look behind me and you'll see them too:
rags and tatters dangling
loosely in the wind.
How they must have snapped and popped
as I crashed blindly through. Stoically,
their mistresses already spin anew.

Still, I wonder as I walk,
what I walk upon, or who—
though what else might I do?
I cannot step unless
I step upon something, and still
I cannot stop my stepping.

August 1

The sun rises noticeably later, now. I arrive early, to a scene from <u>Bambi</u>. The six-point buck walks nonchalantly across the road from Grom Run up the hill to the upper meadow. A doe follows closely, and a fawn follows her. But Disney writes fairy tales—bucks aren't paternal. They mate with their harems, then melt into the woods, solitary. Well, bucks aren't supposed to follow people around, either. This is one iconoclastic fellow.

Grom Run has dwindled to a stony path, just a memory written in damp rocks and dark earth. I'd like to see if the salamanders still lie beneath the rocks, but it seems better not to bother them. Better to let them keep whatever moisture they still cling to.

The woods don't seem so desiccated, though perhaps the drought's effects are more subtle than my eyes are trained to see. Another subtlety I hope to notice is the gradual disappearance of the migrants. So far, I haven't seen signs of that, either. As three robins chase each other through the black cherry trees I do notice that one looks very decrepit, especially around its head. Molting, I presume. But actual departures, from either migration or extinction, seem to be among those quiet, momentous events that no one sees. I suppose that, one night, without fanfare, the thrushes simply fly out of the woods, south. Or the last passenger pigeon dies. A few days later, we realize that we haven't seen a thrush, or a passenger pigeon, for a while. Eventually, we realize that we won't for a few months—or ever.

The woods are quiet at the moment. The activity of early morning has passed. The day is heating up. Such lulls are good opportunities to gaze about more passively, almost meditatively, to see the inconspicuous or to realize the subtle. But for half an hour or so, nothing of note has appeared to me. Finally, there is movement in the bushes. A red squirrel pokes its head out, then walks up the trunk and into the highest branches of a walnut tree. It then casually strolls a broad flat path across the crowns of tulip, hickory, and walnut trees. Or so it must seem to him. To me, it's nightmare material, a wild night of vertigo and falling. But such easy athleticism is just the daily routine in the animal world.

There is more movement in the walnut tree. This time, it's two, or maybe three, yellow-billed cuckoos! Perhaps this is the family of the one that caught caterpillars in the oak tree in May. They're finding some kind of insects up there, but, in typical cuckoo fashion, they don't stay long. Before I've caught my breath, they're gone.

A cardinal gleams bright red against the dark green background. The picture he

142

paints is so common in the woods that one would think it would become a cliché, as hackneyed as a painting on felt. But it hasn't for me. Cardinals never fail to dazzle me.

I'm shaken from my reverie by an irate titmouse that is right in my face, shouting furiously. A chickadee, then a Carolina wren, a robin, and finally a couple of jays join the prosecution, though I still don't know what I've done. I feel rather like Alice after an ill-fated bite of mushroom has sent her towering into the treetops and The Pigeon is circling her head screaming "Serpent! Serpent!" Eventually, they leave, apparently having made some point, and I'm left with the gentle tapping of a woodpecker that has been minding its own business on a nearby branch throughout the whole proceeding.

Another lull begins, and again a spider web appears in an angle of the sun. Drawn across an airy highway traveled by none but the tiny, the main cables and radial threads glisten for only moments, then vanish as the sunlight passes by. But, like the Cheshire cat's grin, one piece of the whole remains: a circular collar of denser threads that hangs, apparently in midair, around the web's invisible center. On this, the web's dark mistress is still at work. Like some angular mechanical monster, she ratchets around the collar—the lips of the trap, I suspect—spinning and spinning. I wonder if this visible circle is the wide end of a funnel, leading to the invisible trap in the middle. Perhaps the grin is more than metaphor.

The lull ends as I walk the path down the hill. Across the valley, probably near the upper meadow, crows have spied an enemy. Their anger flows down the hillside; it seems like the tulip leaves tremble in its vehemence. But the chase runs off in another direction and fades, finally, past my hearing. Into that emptiness, flute music flows from the hillside behind me. It's a startling counterpoint to hatred and tells me, besides, that the wood thrush hasn't left yet! And now the veery and a grackle add their voices—though neither adds much musicality. The veery doesn't, and the grackle can't.

The bee balm along Grom Run has finished flowering. The fuzzy brown heads remind me of the bald pates of dandelions after the seed fluff has flown. The "fuzz", though, consists of long thin tubes that lead to seed nurseries below, I think.

The pond's water level is at least a few inches low: the lily pads stand three or four inches above it. There is no rattle in the overflow drain. There is no outflow. The stream below the pond is as dry and sad as Grom Run. Life does seem pretty normal in and around the pond, though. The cattails are taller than I. Their smooth brown candles, plush. Bullfrogs hump hugely along the shoreline and among the lily pads. Their large brown tadpoles lurk just below the water's surface. Some have legs, already.

I had thought that tadpoles lived on algae, but these are nearly leaping out of the water after something. The slurps and splashes of their hunts send out little rings all across the pond, among the lily pads and midst the algal bloom that floats in the deeper water. Perhaps, along with their legs, they have discovered the carnivores' tastes. Hopefully, those tastes include mosquito larvae.

Mosquitoes must have a tenuous life near this pond. Besides the frogs, swallows, and flycatchers, the pond hosts a variety of dragonflies. Three species seem dominant today. Two are pretty easy to identify: the common whitetail, which is aptly named, and the widow skimmer, whose black and white wings flash all across the pond. The third kind seems to be a pondhawk, but a lot of dragonflies are blue, so that's a guess. The mosquitoes don't care.

"Who cooks for you?" That's a silly question, unless an owl is asking, for that's what barred owls say. It seems unusual to hear an owl hooting during the day, but barred owls seem less constrained by their nocturnal nature than the other species. And so the question keeps rolling out of the woods across the road. I'd love to walk over there, but my morning has passed. I suspect that the crows were there, earlier.

August 7

Yesterday, a cold front passed through, but far too quickly. Some rain fell, but only to tease a parched land, it seemed. A month of such days might revive the streams and meadows. Still, even one chilly morning seems like a reprieve. Mists are rolling across the pond. High above the fog, the sun has just begun to paint the very tips of the highest trees.

I'm guessing that, with the streams gone dry, the pond may serve as an oasis, a watering hole in our little Serengeti. But as I stand watching by my willow, the sun's brush strokes have swept down the hillsides and now sweep over me, and little else has passed. The phoebe hunts from tree to tree, swallows circle and swoop above the water. Tadpoles lurk and circle beneath. Bullfrogs croak all around me; crows call from the distance. A green heron leaped noisily from the cattails. I hadn't seen it till it left. A nuthatch is talking to itself as it pokes and prods among the upper reaches of my willow. This is more like family sitting down to breakfast than adventure on the African plain—a placid morning for all but those that are trying to avoid being breakfast.

The story is the same among the cattails and then up the hill along Grom Run: a placid, pleasant morning that is presenting little to report. I've wondered what sort of news would filter down from heaven, if heaven there be. Perhaps it's like this.

August 14

Rain! Finally! It rattles on the leaves of the canopy over Grom Run so loudly that, if any birds are singing, their melodies are drowning before they reach me. But after weeks—no, months—without it, I'd forgotten how it sounds. Forgotten the heaviness of a gray, wet morning. Forgotten how hope springs up from that heaviness. For drought is a burden, a long chain dragging behind like Marley's cash boxes, for those whose feet touch the earth. But these chains are forged from the desiccated and dying. Sometime in early July, I sickened of the television weather reporters' fatuous glee as they announced yet another week of blue skies and heat. Today, as they groan, I'll dance.

Not that this is "the mother of all rains". So far, not much water is actually reaching the ground, and the drop that lands on my nose has already skied down the green slopes of dozens of leaves. Above me, the leaves recoil as drops fall on them, then shiver as the water slides down to the uttermost tips, gathers itself, and leaps into the abyss to be caught, once again, on a thirsty green palm. It seems like the woods, not the sky, is raining.

Some stretches of Grom Run have regained their voices, though they can only whisper weakly so far. Little trickles wet the rocks. Where they gather in small pools, water striders skate again. So somehow they survived when the water went away. When I turn a rock over, a salamander wriggles hastily away, dives into a rivulet and under a rock. A little farther down the run, the stream disappears into the stones. Its streambed becomes a stony path again, as though the thirsty earth has given it a taste of freedom, then gulped it down. But a hundred yards down that path, the waters re-emerge, and stronger. We've been told that still waters run deep. This little one does, too. There's more to Grom Run than a casual glance will see.

A large black cherry tree has fallen across the path up the hill. One long-dead limb, rusty brown and covered with the pale green mouths of decay, fell across a young hickory sapling. The young tree snapped at its base. The dead old branch lays over the younger almost affectionately, like a lover's arm.

The rain diminishes. Above the canopy, the clouds may have wrung themselves dry, but beneath, the trees still drip. Mist rises from the woodland floor. A sunbeam falls on a droplet that hasn't yet leaped from its leaf, and so the beam is splattered into a glittering rainbow. Had it fallen into a diamond, it couldn't have done better.

A vireo begins to sing, then a cardinal joins. In the quiet interludes, a gentle snoring wafts through the leaves. A blue-winged warbler may be singing up there, but I can't see it. Then a sharper, more complicated song cuts through. Probably either a hooded warbler or a Carolina wren; I can't tell which.

Suddenly, the sylvan sanctity is trampled beneath the thudding of tired feet as a girls' cross-country team labors up the hill. This is, after all, a working woods. The variety of people that comes here, and the multitude of views they see, would surely amaze me. But if my flashback to August Practices Past, to sweat and aching muscles long ago, reflects these young women's minds, they're only enduring at the moment, and seeing very little.

Now, shortly after they've passed, a bit of mockery from the woods: three deer lope effortlessly up the same hill. Straight up the hill. They don't use the path.

Down the path in the other direction, most of the bee balm seems to have disappeared. The remnants have brown burnt-out tops on nearly naked stems. White snakeroot, I think, has taken its place. When it blossoms, I'll know.

And again, for contrast, a tiger swallowtail butterfly sips at the mud in a boot print on the path. It seems to define fragility and beauty. But the paper-thin yellow wings quiver in the ecstasy of wet earth.

I was too harsh in my diatribe on anthropomorphism; we all draw lines, often unconsciously. I've drawn one between mud and beauty. I should have known better. Forgive me, gardeners.

August 21

There is a fortunate fork in the path near the edge of the upper meadow. A deer's brown rump, partly obscured by bushes, switches its white tail on the path to the right. I watch quietly for a while, then take the path to the left. This path dives into a grassy ravine overgrown in cherry, dogwood, maple, and other second-growth woodland. It is also currently occupied by a spotted fawn. We come face to face as I walk into the trees. At the moment, it's standing in the path a few yards from me, watching me write these notes. This may be the child of the buck with the attitude. Surely, those big brown eyes are windows into innocence. I sense a poem in this meeting, but I've grown too worldly to write it. I want the fawn to leave. That rump on the other path was probably Mom's, and I'd rather not stand between them. Minutes pass. Finally, the youngster drifts into the underbrush.

I wait for a few respectful minutes more, then walk to the meadow's edge. Spring was noisy here, as the sun rose above the dogwoods and cherry trees. Today, as the sun rises, few birds sing. There's a towhee in the distance and squirrels, both fox and red species, run in the trees above. And now deer step into the meadow where that other path enters. A large buck, at least six points and no longer in velvet, leads four or five others, but warily. The leaves hang limply, but there must be a slight southerly breeze—soon they turn back into the woods. When I turn around, a coolness on my face bespeaks that breeze.

The "old" meadow, the sections that weren't sprayed and replanted, is now rather sparse and brown. The orchard grass has dried up. Queen Anne's Lace and Canada Thistle are blooming there now. The "new" meadow, though, is lushly green with knee-high—no, waist-high—grass bowing with heavy seed heads. Mullein plants stand out like sentinel towers. And the grass is drenched in dew! The bright droplets I took for granted in May are a delightful surprise in August.

The little copse around the old windmill is fairly active. Two song sparrows sit near me, as does a hummingbird, for a too-brief moment. A flycatcher hunts from a branch higher up. But the real center of activity is the line of bushes and the sycamore in the middle of the meadow. A flock of small birds is swarming about the tree. They may be migrating, but they're too far away to identify. So I wade the new meadow to get closer.

The birds are cedar waxwings. The flock is pretty big, at least twenty, and they're loudly jockeying for the best places on the tree until I arrive. I seem to ruin it for them, so they leave. This may be the flock that I saw near here in January, so it isn't likely that this is a migratory gathering.

Perhaps, if I stand quietly at the base of the tree, they'll come back. And while that spot is well protected by brambles and poison ivy, the whole meadow lays stretched out around it. It's a great observation point, as the birds know well.

I hope it wasn't too busy for the orioles' nest; the nest is gone now. It was so high in the tree and so far out among the small branches that it seemed pretty safe from the larger climbing predators like cats and coons. I doubt that a snake would knock the nest down. Crows? Maybe. It was so very visible. Maybe a hiker collected it after the chicks had fledged.

Although the waxwings left as I arrived, many other birds didn't. Bluebirds are in the tall grass. A pair of phoebes pass through, then three red-winged blackbirds and a house finch. At the tip of a bramble bush, a molting indigo bunting is preening in the sun. He's still very blue and very pretty, but he's also rather ragged-looking, especially around his head and breast. As he preens, a fluffy under-feather floats north on the freshening breeze. One dark night, when his transformation is complete, he'll rise, chittering to others of his kind, and float the other way.

I'd never thought much about the molt until this year. Now I see it all around me. The basics of the molt seem simple: feathers are critical to flight, warmth, camouflage, and mating rituals, and they wear out. Virtually all birds replace most or all of their feathers during the "pre-basic" molt (to produce "basic" plumage) in late summer, after the mating and family raising season and before migration and winter. Food and cover are abundant then. Most birds also undergo a second, the "pre-alternate", molt before the spring breeding season. This molt is often partial. Beyond these basic principles, the species to species variation is bewildering. For example, although molting does use up a lot of energy, most birds don't seem to be particularly vulnerable during the process. Male ducks, though, are flightless and quite vulnerable for a part of their molt. There's too much to know. So, on this as well as most other bird-related subjects, I find myself consulting Sibley a lot.

I suspect that I won't see the bunting again till April. But for the goldfinches, it might as well be spring right now. They passed on the fruits of May to await the purple thistle blossoms of August. Now the thistles are in bloom and the meadow is full of goldfinches. Their flight is always a scalloped course from here to there: several wing strokes to an apogee, a swoop down to the bottom of the arc, and more wing strokes. But, I'd been told, during the breeding season, the males exaggerate that flight. And they do. The fellow in front of me arrived after a series of arcs that went from near stalls at 20 or 30 feet into dives almost into the ground. It wasn't an efficient way to travel, but it sure was spectacular. Somehow, he managed to land on the very tip of a mullein without breaking his arc. Now he's looking around to see if anyone was impressed.

And perhaps she was. I can't tell. She shares, with a bumblebee, a thistle blossom that has partly gone to seed. Apparently preoccupied with lunch, she plunges her stubby bill down to her eyes in fluff. She probes a bit, and finally emerges with seed and parachute. A sharp bite snips off the latter; she munches the former. Downwind from her, a long line of seedless parachutes floats impotent on the breeze. Or so it seems. The abundance of thistles says that she must miss some. And the abundance of goldfinches says that she didn't miss his flight, either.

August is also the time for the cicadas. One lands on a branch above my head: a big black bug with transparent wings. No orange eye that I can see, certainly no red stripe. The annual cicadas are less colorful, but just as loud as their seventeen-year relatives. This one doesn't sing, though. It's just passing through.

Suddenly, immediately overhead, a red-tailed hawk leaves, too, floating through a swirling wind of chittering swallows and finches. Apparently, the hawk was sitting upstairs in the attic while I stood in the basement below. We just don't get to know our neighbors! The hawk and its whirlwind drift west, down the length of the meadow. Soon, the swallows and finches return, victorious.

All of the swallows are barn swallows. Squadrons of them have been swooping above the meadow all morning. I've looked for the tree swallows that nested here, but haven't seen any. Perhaps they've left already. It seems early, though.

Barn swallows are mostly blue and orange, with deeply forked tails and long narrow wings. They nest in colonies on rafters or similar structures in nests built of mud. At Latodami, they fly in and out of the barn all day. Male tree swallows are an iridescent blue-green on top, white-breasted, with only slightly forked tails; females are markedly drabber. They're cavity nesters and won't tolerate the presence of one bane of cavity nesters, house sparrows. Unlike bluebirds, they're aggressive enough to chase the sparrows away. They don't mind bluebirds. So many bluebird aficionados place bird boxes in pairs, one for the bluebirds and one for their protectors.

Born to catch flying insects, their flight is marvelous to watch. To them, air isn't just a medium to cross over—it's where they live. In describing their flight, I've overused swooping, curling, and diving, but that's what they do. A similar bird, the chimney swift, is so adapted for flight that it can't perch. Instead, it flies continuously, returning to cling to vertical surfaces at its roost at night. The swallows aren't so radical: barn swallows perch in rows on power lines around the barn, while the tree swallows perch on promontories all across the meadow.

As I watched for tree swallows, the ghost of a kingbird slipped through a breach in the brambles. This has seemed like a good place for kingbirds, but I hadn't seen any. Now one sits on a mullein spike nearby, peering around for insects. The hawk has returned. Now it's perched on the tip of a cherry branch at the southeast corner of the meadow. It, too, is peering around. The hawk's prey is larger, but the two birds' style and intent, regardless of size, are the same. The hawk sees something, focuses more narrowly below, and glides down into the woods and out of sight.

It's now late morning, nearly cloudless and getting hot. On the way home, at the edge of the meadow, several clouds of midges swirl madly in the sunlight. This has to be a mating ritual. At first, they're spinning balls of specks that hover near eye level. They seem coherent, rather like a globular cluster of stars, held together by the gravity of sex. But these are evanescent clusterings. At a signal, perhaps a gust of wind, the balls disperse and the specks float singly, like plankton, swept here and there by the currents. Perhaps they only catch their breath. For then, again, they seem to fall into a vortex in the air. Cyclones of motes reform as more and more are drawn, or race on tiny wings, into the dance. Soon they're swirling madly in the sunlight once again.

At first, I thought that such tiny creatures must be slaves to the vagaries of winds. Now I see that the life that blows through all of us gusts, even in such minims, stronger by far than air.

August 27

Still, while others chortle at the long, long train of "perfect days," I scan the empty blue for signs of rain. If I could, I'd leap up into it to wring ten drops of precious rain from those few puffs that float across the desiccated sky. Or dance a Shawnee prayer, but I fear those rhythms died two hundred years ago.

Some rain has fallen—a day or two. We need a month. But Grom's stream is running once again—well, creeping anyway. It trickles and it puddles.

Calls of towhees, jays, and flickers and the chatter of an unhappy squirrel trickle, too, into a quiet August morning. Just as my eyelids droop, Mom coon and her three pups appear from the barberries and ferns, march in single file across a long-dead tree that leans across the stream, and vanish once again into the barberries and snakeroot on my side. The kids are nearly grown. No matter. Mom leads; they follow. This road must be as familiar to them as is Brown Road to locals who jog it every day: the four raccoons walk it with the nonchalance of those who walk it every day, unchallenged. Perhaps they haven't heard the rumors of a black bear in the park.

Bee balm is now a memory and skeletal stalks scattered through a patch of white snakeroot. Those tiny white blooms glow pale white in the dim woodland green. A few more voices filter down through the leaves: nuthatch, Carolina wren, and veery. I haven't heard the wood thrushes for a long time. I suppose they've left—the rainforests are so far away. I hope they find their winter homes are still standing when they arrive. The trees are falling fast.

On my way across Brown Road and up the hill to the upper meadow, I brushed against a burr-like vine. Now I'm a major carrier of prickly little green seeds. As I preen, halfway up the hill, a hawk looms suddenly at eye level. There's no time to blink; there's hardly time to snap my head around to see its tail feathers disappear among the trees behind me. Sharp-shinned or Cooper's hawk?

Maybe. No buteo (*large soaring hawk, like the red-winged*) could fly through the woods like that, and I didn't see the white rump of a Northern Harrier. Jays are calling from its wake—a little late. Perhaps their chatter is a nervous reaction to the passage of the swift hand of Death. That, surely, is its real name.

At the top of the hill, at the base of a large pine, the feathered half of a fiberglass arrow lies nearly covered by twigs and duff. And the other half? That's the one that would tell the tale. I suppose the jays screamed, too, on the day that shaft flew through.

The younger woods at the top of the hill are quiet, too, but the meadow is busy. The mullein towers are ringed with little yellow flowers and, often, capped by a bird. It seems like flight, itself, would give a fellow a really good overview of the meadow. Evidently, though, there's still much to be said for a solid perch on a pinnacle.

There are lots of perches: mullein, the apple tree and windmill across the meadow, the bisecting line of bushes, and the sycamore above me. There are also lots of birds. A small flock of female indigo buntings is an unusual sight to me. The field guide says they form flocks for their migration. Perhaps I won't see them again until spring. Phoebes, field sparrows, catbirds, and barn swallows will leave, too, but not so soon. They're busy eating berries in the bushes or diving for bugs, depending on their niche. A hummingbird lands above me, perches briefly, then darts after a passing swallow. One might as well shoot an arrow at a passing F-16—the swallow draws a swift "S" in the air above the mullein and the hummingbird zips by like a small black bolt. It pierces only oxygen, nitrogen, and, finally, apple tree. But I wonder how the swallow offended it, and how I can avoid that offense. When dealing with hummingbirds, I suspect that quicker is better than bigger.

Size doesn't seem to impress hummingbirds much.

Of all the birds in the meadow today, the goldfinches are most numerous and most active. We all follow some siren's song. The singers, for the goldfinches, must be the thistles. At any given moment, two or three finches are perched on or pulling apart a thistle blossom. One male flies distractedly from thistle to thistle and finally into a bush, pursued by a duller finch that could be a female, but is probably a young bird that doesn't want to feed itself quite yet. Each time it lands by the male, it quivers its wings, as in the "feed me" routine.

But even more fascinating than the goldfinches are the butterflies. At least six species are fluttering among the thistles in front of me: the little white "cabbage whites," a small yellow sulfur species, yellow and black "tiger swallowtails," predominantly brown swallowtails, predominantly black swallowtails, and an orange and black fritillary (probably a "great spangled fritillary"). The brown swallowtail looked like a "spicebush swallowtail," but what was it doing on a thistle? The field guide says they only feed on spicebushes and sassafras.

The good news from all this is that I've learned to differentiate among butterflies. A year ago, they all looked the same to me. The bad news is that I still know very little about them. And the lesson? If I'm to learn more, I'll have to improve my field drawings.

But beyond the knowledge, beyond the detail, there is, for anyone who will look, the beauty. Immediately in front of me, a tiger swallowtail gently flutters as it walks the violet lips of a newly opening thistle blossom. Fragile film of black and yellow, soft purple tufts, green stem and hard stern thorns—the colors and contrasts paint their work of art in the circle of my binoculars. A photographer with a very long and professional-looking lens is stalking the meadow today, too. I hope he captured a vision like this. *(He did. He took the cover photo.)*

As I walk through the grasses, every step sends a spray of fleeing grasshoppers rattling into the meadow around and ahead of me. Those that leap straight ahead just have to leap again in a step or two. Those that realize the beauties of obliqueness first are also first to rest as I tromp by.

In the grassy ravine that falls down the hill toward my car, a small (two- or three-inches in diameter) rotten limb lays across the deer path I'm walking. A section of it has been torn apart. If this were much larger, it would say "Bear." But this might just have been stepped on hard. I didn't see any bear tracks in the soft ground by Grom Run. Still, the raccoons and I should walk less casually this fall.

Farther down in the ravine, a deer is resting beneath the trees. Resting, not dozing. She watches me walk by; I notice her as little as possible. She's probably too comfortable to dash off without good cause. The air is getting warm. A nap seems like a good idea.

September

Acorns

Scattered on the sidewalk,
crunched by passing cars,
they lay as if God's fruitcart overturned,
and He just walked away.
But though God might disdain
to procreate suburban oaks—

I, at least, did not. Gingerly I stepped
around those eggs of immortality.
I scooped them up in handfuls,
walked home with bulging jeans,
and smiling, pressed the future
into the fringes of my lawn.

Three years ago, that was,
and not a one has grown.
Four foot tall and thriving, though,
stand two I didn't plant.
They are, I think, the legacies
of absent-minded squirrels.

September 5

Two nights ago, the tall clouds marched in darkness, flashed and crashed for an hour or two, threw down rain in arrows and spears—half an inch, we're told—then stalked away to flicker and mutter in the east. Such grudging acquiescence to our prayers. I wonder what we've done to offend them so. It's the CO_2, I suppose.

In any case, half an inch is nearly nothing. Not enough to send a rivulet rattling down the pond's outflow drain to wet the rocks downstream. Not enough to cover up the cracked and drying mud flats. As the water level drops, the lily pads advance. They almost own the pond. Yet they lose as much as they gain as the pond shrinks. As the water melts away, they're left with only mud, their toes dry up, and their turgid pancake leaves curl into brown, over-baked blintzes.

Still, tadpoles slurp and leap among the lily pads. A green heron squawks in a tree above me, and a great blue heron stalks the shoreline. Two mallard hens wade the edge, placidly shoveling slime with their noses. A sandpiper pokes more delicately at some tiny mud creatures. My first thought is that this may be the same solitary sandpiper that passed through on its way north from the tropics, and now stops again on its way south. Perhaps it is. But it seems more likely to be a spotted sandpiper in winter plumage. If it would fly, I could tell. It seems happy enough where it is, though, and my interest in the color of its tail feathers doesn't seem sufficient reason to bother it.

Deer have been here earlier, and raccoons. Generations of coons have learned to walk lightly on the ooze, but not so deer. Those sharp hooves leap like ballet slippers among the oak leaves, but here, they slice right through. I imagine a doe, a vision of grace on solid ground, slogging through muck up to her ankles for her morning drink and blushing as the goo sucks noisily with every careful step.

As the morning progresses, the parade of birds passes through. It started with crows; it usually does. Then jays, catbirds, Carolina wrens, flickers, nuthatches, titmice, chickadees, a hairy woodpecker, and a yellow-headed warbler, briefly seen. A coopers hawk (or sharp-shinned) flashes through, too, from the direction of the pine woods along Brown Road. I wonder if it's the same hawk, on the same trajectory, that I saw on my last outing. It's about the same time, too.

Goldenrod bows along the path back to my car. The warbler's passage stops me, but a catbird urges me on. Apparently, I'm standing too near a silky dogwood that belongs to him. Blue and white berries hang in clusters from it. He snatches a couple, harangues me, grabs another berry... He's torn between love of the berries and dislike of me. So I simplify his life—I leave.

September 9

The waning of summer never surprises me, but the advent of autumn always does. I don't know why. Nevertheless, the autumnal equinox is upon us. In June, 5:30 AM was too late to head for the woods; now it's too early.

This is another morning of dramatic backlighting. East of me, along the Braille Trail, the oaks are black sharp-edged pillars supporting a green roof. Just above my head, a wasp has landed on a maple leaf. Later, he'll be invisible from below, but now his silhouette is a fantastic stick figure lurching about on a light green stage. The leaves around him have faded to light yellow-green, spotted with brown, like liver spots, and tinged with the first blushes of autumn. Many are bedraggled, riddled, and chewed. Last year's oak leaves litter the floor. Soon they'll have company.

A lively troupe still sports about, largely unseen, up among those old leaves, though. The morning is bright and loud, with jays, crows, a hooded warbler, song sparrows, chickadees, nuthatches, Carolina wrens, three kinds of woodpeckers, a veery, robins, a vireo, towhees, red and fox squirrels, and chipmunks. Two red-bellied woodpeckers chip away at an oak close by. One seems to have finished its part of the oak—rather like finishing the Internet—and flies off. The other seems startled, looks all around, and then follows. A red squirrel clings upright to the back side of a sapling nearby. Poking out from the left side, his eyes and ears draw lines that converge on...me. His body is hidden, but below those eyes, on the right side of the tree, his tail flips angrily. Rather than chuckle and annoy him even more, I find something very interesting higher up another tree. When I look back, he's gone.

My condescension is soon rewarded. The shriek of some poor creature *in extremis* slices through the woods, and I find myself peering up the hill from behind my tree, the whites of my eyes lost in large, round, black pupils. Had I a tail, it would be tucked in safely. No bird could make that cry. A cat? A squirrel? A coon, perhaps? Nothing moves among the dry leaves on the hillside. Sound is suspended. Chatters and whistles hang frozen just beyond a hundred hidden glottises.

Well, almost all. A few seconds later, a blue jay slides through the trees from that direction, bubbling and tootling.

I've said it before. I say it again. Blue jays smirk.

The chatters and whistles flow again. A few crisp leaves clatter to the ground. A groundhog appears as a lump on a log. It refreezes, eyes on me. But I'm far more interested in the warblers. This hillside is part of the hunting circuit of a mixed flock of small birds. They've passed through twice before, and now the Carolina wrens that seem to be the vanguard are approaching again. Here they are, chattering on a fallen tree trunk. One is molting and ragged, but still loud. Here is the red flash of a cardinal. And here are at least two species of warbler. One skips across my view on twigs of bushes and bark of tree trunks. She's a movie run too fast, mostly a blur of yellow. But she's almost certainly a female or immature hooded or Wilson's warbler. The second warbler is yellow, too, but has distinct wing bars, an eye stripe, and faint lines on its breast. It does stay in one place longer, but its place is a very leafy bush. It bobs and ducks through the leaves like a reluctant fan dancer. My best guess is that it's an immature blackburnian warbler, but that's just a guess. It's fun to watch, no matter what it is.

Autumn bird identification is notoriously difficult, at least for those of us who aren't expert. Many males do change to a duller plumage, but apparently a bigger problem is that a large proportion of fall birds are immature, and haven't yet developed their species' distinctive markings.

And why all this fuss about warblers? In <u>Anatomy of a Fisherman</u>, Robert Traver tried to answer that question—about all the fuss about fly-fishing for trout. I suspect that the birder's answer would be similar because warblers and trout are viewed as the aristocracies of their respective kinds. They're beautiful, they're elusive, they aren't easy to identify (read "catch," for trout)—that's a trembling beginning. Most of all, to paraphrase Traver, I love warblers because I love to be where warblers are. To their great endangerment, neither warblers nor trout love civilization.

Like Grom Run, the stream that flows through the Braille Trail is just a trickle. Still, the little marsh where the streams meet seems healthy. Joe Pye weed and jewelweed are in bloom. The cattails are taller than I am, and beginning to turn fluffy. But the milkweeds interest me most. I'm looking for monarch butterfly caterpillars, especially after the catastrophic die-off in Mexico when temperatures plummeted on their mountain last winter. These milkweeds look rather tattered, but their pods haven't opened yet. Nonetheless, they support a variety of orange bug-life. There are several clusters of small orange beetles—smaller and narrower than ladybugs. They seem to be sunning themselves. Black and orange "box elder" bugs walk the stalks singly. Several small, symmetrical, orange and black caterpillars lay on the leaves. There's one thin, delicate wasp, black with a bright orange tail. But no monarchs.

I'd read that this orange motif runs through the population of insects whose life cycles are closely tied to the milkweed and its bitter juice, that it's a sign to would-be predators that this bug would be an evil-tasting meal. Monarchs are just the most famous of this clan. I'd never looked for it before, but it seems to be true.

On the other hand, ladybugs are swarming all over the jewelweed.

All of this area, by the way, belongs to a hummingbird. He likes to oversee his domain from a perch in an overhanging willow. But every few minutes, a competitor bruises his tranquility. Then duty calls and off he zooms. For several exhilarating seconds, two angry darts buzz the cattails in tight, vicious loops until the interloper—I presume—draws a straight line back into the woods—with a long needle among his tail feathers urging him on. The owner returns to his willow twig to preen and contemplate the autumn sunshine.

In the pond, the other end on the scale of loveliness is cruising the edge of the lily pads. Her head is the broken end of a knobby branch, her shell a round lump in the water, and her tail a serrated relic from the days of dinosaurs. Even from the land, in bright daylight, the snapping turtle's silent passage lays subliminal lines among my neurons that will surely resurface in the long dark hours of the night. And now she slips out of sight to reappear as a slight rustling among the lily pads—with jaws like a steel trap. The lily pads wriggle slightly, innocently, in a line that would intersect the bank several yards from me…and then the wriggling ceases. I find I've stepped, involuntarily, a few feet up the bank.

At last I break my reverie and walk farther along the bank. Suddenly, a bullfrog shouts. We both jump. But his leap takes him into the lily pads; mine takes me to my car.

September 17

The sycamore is raining on me this foggy morning. The humidity is 100%; the visibility in the upper meadow is a hundred feet or so. The line of autumn olives and brambles is a subdued gray-green mass that recedes to a dim silhouette and, gradually, into shapes only imagined in the whiteness. Close around me, dewdrops form and drip from the brambles and poison ivy. And from the sycamore. Plap. Plap. Plap on my hat. Birds flutter in the bushes, but I can't see who they are. Geese gabble invisibly above me; I suspect that they fly in sunshine above this very low cloud. Voices of robins, jays, and a towhee call from the gloom. From farther come the human sounds: distant hammering, the beeping of a backing truck, the white hum of traffic.

The sun must be climbing higher and higher, but this cloud is too heavy, too resolute, to dissipate. A chilly north wind blows stronger, but the mists remain. At last I tire of being wrapped so tightly in such a small gray world. Perhaps there is more to see in the woods. The crows and jays seem to think so.

First, I have to cross the meadow. The grass in the new planting has matured and is a sea of fuzzy tan squirrel-tails bowing heavy with dew. It seems better not to wade that sea; I go around. The old areas are thick with the white flowers of snakeroot and catfoot. Some thistles are still green and blooming, but more and more are turning brown and bristly. Thistledown lies sodden around them and hangs out from prickly brown pods like rifled pockets. Most of the bluebird houses have been taken down; their poles still stand above the grasses, but now they look like the remnants of a lost and wayward fence. The thick velvety leaves of the mullein have withered to brittle brown husks. The stalks still stand above the grasses, rather like the birdhouse poles, but reminiscent of cacti. An orb spider has strung a beautifully round web between a mullein stalk and a bramble stem. But I doubt the mistress will catch much in her lovely trap this morning—the mists have drawn it in bold white lines upon the air. The threads are strings of tiny pearls of dew, drooping with the weight—and oh so visible to all. Function has succumbed to art, if only for a little while.

Catfoot, or sweet everlasting, may be a misidentification. I'm told that dominant wildflowers in the old part of the meadow include pearly everlasting, blue vervain, St. Johnswort, ironweed, moth mullein, the common mullein I've talked about, bladder campion, and, of course, the thistles and goldenrod. But those buds sure do remind me of a cat's toes.

I've also learned that the dominant grasses in the new planting are giant foxtail and yellow foxtail...and that neither was supposed to be part of the new planting. They're "volunteers" that do well when they have little competition, and the cutting/herbicidal treatment killed their competition. Meg Scanlon says that, if you look, you can see two species of blue stem and several other species of grasses and wildflowers tucked in among the foxtails. But something went wrong with the planting, and these intended species didn't dominate. In time, they will. And, to help them, there may be a second planting in the spring.

The woods rise before me, tall dark forms at first, and then just dripping trees. But as I leave, at the base of the hill, I find that the sun has finally broken through. The fog is in tatters and dissipating quickly. Too bad, really. We need the water so desperately. Grom Run is once again just a moist rocky path.

The drought casts an anxious shadow that only fades in the morning sun. It never wholly disappears, but life goes on. Robins, in a flock now, are chasing each other through the treetops. Nuts still in their green hulls lie at the base of the shaggy-barked hickory trees. A red squirrel is gathering them, one at a time, into some hideaway. A chipmunk has the temerity to think they might be shared. Red squirrels aren't known for their sociability. The chase leaves a trail of dry leaves fluttering back down to earth in a wide arc from the hickory to my foot and down the hill into the barberry bushes. Soon, the squirrel returns, runs to the highest point on a fallen maple, and chatters long and loudly—a victory cry, as well as a warning. Then the squirrel goes back to its gathering and, while it's away, the chipmunk returns quietly. Soon it, too, leaves with a nut.

The drought's shadow mutes my amusement at what would normally be a mock-competition. This year, at least, the business of collecting food for winter may be very serious. The crop of nuts seems meager, the result, I suspect, of extreme weather: spring was cold, wet, and late, while summer was hot and dry. A hard winter may well be dying time for many chipmunks and squirrels.

September 24

Autumn has officially—and actually—returned. The pond is steaming, the temperature is 44°, and until the sun climbs above the hills, at least, I'm wearing a jacket. The pond itself looks rather sad. The water level is at least a foot low. The lily pads have shriveled and sunk; all that remains of them are forlorn stalks that protrude like the broken masts of sunken ships. Cattail stalks are turning brown, and their lovely velvet candles are bursting into white fluff. It's just the next step in their march to overrun the pond and turn it into marsh, all in the natural order of things, but rather disheveled.

The kingfisher rattling over doesn't seem affected. The low water level may be a problem for the muskrat, but the quick V he's drawing in the water suggests he's more concerned with me, right now. He bows before a doorway in some roots and the pond slurps him home. The moon, just past full, wavers in the ripples of his passing.

Above, flocks of geese are drawing their own V's across the sky. Several groups of twenty to thirty have passed westward, gabbling loudly among themselves.

The geese and I have this in common today: we're just passing through as quickly as possible. My passing is too quick for a mallard hen that nuzzles the duckweed. She flaps wetly to the other side of the pond. On Latodami's gravel drive, two of the young coons are arriving on their morning round. Suddenly, we're eye to eye. They slip into the bushes and up the hill. They're young, but no longer naive: I reach their turnoff seconds later, but they've disappeared.

And now I've reached my destination: the marsh and woods around the convergence of Grom Run and the Braille Trail stream. I've found, as the year has passed, that there's almost always something going on here. There's something in the variety of food sources and types of trees, the running water, the snags and dead branches riddled with woodpecker holes, and probably even the thickets of barberry that attracts both a variety of year-round residents and some rather exotic summer campers. Consider that many of the warblers, thrushes, tanagers, and cuckoos fly thousands of miles from South and Central America every year to arrive here! Tagging studies show that this isn't a random choice; birds return to their places of birth, year after year, to raise their families—unless, of course, someone decides to "develop" that place. Then, generally, they die. But that, I trust, won't happen at Latodami, and in February, in some South American jungle, a tanager will get an overwhelming urge to fly to—northern Pittsburgh!

Today, as I stalk semi-quietly into the woods, two hermit thrushes meet me by a willow tree. They chirp at me for a while, then move on. Black walnut trees grow nearby. Below one, a red squirrel has found a nut, still in its green husk, and wants to take it somewhere by the high route. The nut is as big as the squirrel's head, and rather heavy. The squirrel is about three feet up a sapling when, suddenly, it flips over, as though someone has just added one brick too many to the load, and races down the tree as fast as its feet will move. It collects itself, then tries again, with the same result. It flips over like some kind of overloaded lever, races down the tree only slightly more slowly than gravity urges, thinks about it for a moment, then rustles away among the fallen leaves, still lugging the nut.

Among the rhythms in the activity in the woods, one of the most obvious is the passage of flocks of mixed species of small birds. In Latodami, chickadees, cardinals, titmice, nuthatches, downy woodpeckers, kinglets and Carolina wrens forage together throughout the year, except during the nesting season. During the winter, they're joined by juncoes; during the summer, many of the warblers fly with them. The multiplicity of watchful eyes surely makes flying with a flock safer. Also, combining different hunting techniques is, apparently, helpful to all. Woodpeckers tend to move up a tree trunk, nuthatches move down, chickadees and titmice work through the smaller branches, and juncoes are ground feeders. I don't know whether they prefer different bugs or if, since they look at the trees from different angles, they simply don't see the same bugs. Unlike the two hummingbirds that battled for this area, the different species in the mixed flock don't seem to be in direct competition. The hummingbirds clearly were: both wanted the nectar from a fixed number of flowers, and there wasn't enough for both.

If you sit still long enough, they'll pass by several times. I presume that, like all hunters and gatherers, they've found and are following a circuit that offers the most food at that particular time of year. They don't usually stay in one spot long. You can hear the lively chatter of their approach. Suddenly, they're above and all around, up and down and through the trees and bushes. Then, like the quick broom of a maid's cursory sweeping, they're gone. I'm trying to time their circuit today, but keep being diverted. It seems like thirty to forty minutes per round.

I'm unusually sedentary today because of the warblers in the flock. There are at least five species: hooded, yellow, black-throated green, Nashville, and one that I won't even guess at. Each time the flock passes through, I see something I didn't see before—an eye ring, an eye ring and wing-bars, no wing-bars—and wonder whether it's another species or just another detail on the same bird. Each time, I add a little more detail to a sketch, but never with the certainty that it was the same bird. Perhaps on the next passage, it will be clearer...

So here I stand, exuberant and bewildered. For just a few minutes, little yellow birds flicker among the leaves. Yellow flashes in a black cherry: eye ring, yes; wing-bars, yes; what else—gone. Higher up, another flash: no markings underneath; wing-bars, can't tell; oops—vanished. Over in the willow: no eye ring; no wing-bars; tan on the head; can't see white on the tail—she's gone. Soon I feel like I'm staring into the birdwatcher's version of alphabet soup. But if someone were to see me now, they'd probably write: black binoculars above; broad grin below—must be a birdwatcher!

For experts, a quick peek is probably enough. But for those of us just a step or two beyond the guidebooks, some glue on the twigs would help. Warbler identification is difficult enough in May, but the leafiness and subdued markings of autumn make it a real sport. Yes, it's either glue on the twigs or twice as much tape on all the ripped guidebook pages.

I need to remember that, for me, warbler identification is a sport. For the warblers, their autumn hunt is as serious as the squirrel's nut gathering. Studies have shown that, the more fat a migratory bird can accumulate before it begins the flight, the better its chances for survival are. The norm for migratory songbirds just before migration appears to be 30-50% of their weight in fat. The norm for non-migratory birds is about a tenth of that. Of course, birds flying over land can replenish if a storm or strong headwind depletes their reserves. They fall behind in the race to claim the best nesting or wintering location and face increased likelihood of predation, but these setbacks aren't necessarily fatal. Storms at sea are another matter. No one knows how many birds fall into the Gulf of Mexico during such storms. Those that make it come to shore in "fallouts": tens of thousands of exhausted birds plummeting thousands of feet to earth to rest and replenish. For birdwatchers, such an event is the spectacle of a lifetime; for the birds, it's a calamity. If their dive takes them into habitat with good cover and food, they can replenish and be on their way in a few days. But that habitat must be within about 25 miles of the shoreline, or they won't reach it. Unfortunately, on the northward migration at least, those 25 miles are prime locations for condominium developments and biologically sterile tree farms.

Before I dive into despair, it's best that I watch for the flock's next pass. The birds seem healthy; they're certainly active, and they—no, we—face death at every moment anyway. It would be a shame to waste life worrying. The birds don't say this, they do it: "Do what you can, then carry on."

Here comes a fox squirrel with a hickory nut in its mouth. It rustles through the leaves beneath the barberry bushes, nearly over my foot, and down into the willows.

There's always something going on here.

September 28

The ragged end of Hurricane Isadore is drifting off to Albany this morning. For two days, she's run a bucket brigade from New Orleans to Cleveland and points east, and we're grateful—in spite of the damage she might have done to the southward migration. Rainfalls of ten and twelve inches south of us were too much, too fast, with attendant flooding and misery, of course, but the one or two inches here were just breakfast after a long, long night. The cracked earth gaped for her drizzles and downpours like kittens in the barn as the farmer starts his milking.

So this morning I'm walking our little section of the watershed to see what Isadore has wrought.

Immediately, I find that the outlet stream below the pond is flowing again. The flow isn't a spring freshet, but it is steady. The meadow grasses that were marching into it have wet feet now. They'll have to march back out.

The level in the pond is nearly normal, only an inch or two low, perhaps. There's enough to rattle over the concrete dam and into the outlet stream. As I approached the pond, a great blue heron was circling above, and as I arrived, a pair of wood ducks left. Two mallard hens and one truly odd duck stayed. No puddle duck, it dives for long seconds to emerge many yards away, as though this were some deep Alaskan bay. A bufflehead? But no, it's far too big and the markings are wrong. It doesn't look like anything I know. So I draw a picture in my notebook and hope for later wisdom.

He was a hooded merganser with his crest folded back. In most of the field guides, the crest is raised. That changes the shape of the white marking behind his head and confused me. But, swimming in a little pond all alone in September, he probably felt no need to strut. He wouldn't be considered uncommon in the larger, deeper lakes, but he is in North Park. I had never seen one.

A white-throated sparrow flits in the bushes ahead of me as I leave the pond. It's just arriving; this is probably the southern terminus of its migration. So we lose a lot in autumn, but we gain some, too.

So silently into the sodden woods. A red-tailed hawk soars above, and when it has gone, a fox squirrel flicks its tail at me until it concludes that I'm just not paying any attention. Jays are screeching at something up the hill. Carolina wrens call loudly all around, two downy woodpeckers tap at the trees. Now is the time for the small birds to pass through, but after a couple of nuthatches, that's all. The warblers may have vanished into the night. The south-bound winds of incoming high pressure zones do offer an extra wing to ride on.

A red squirrel runs down a log with a large walnut. But this squirrel—the same one, probably, but wiser—doesn't try to carry it up the sapling as before. This nut goes into a hole under the log. As minutes pass, a series of acorns dives into that same hole.

Towhees are whistling at something in the barberries, and now "something" turns into a gray cat in an opening. It slides down the hill, low-slung and silent.

Periodically, Meg sets live-traps to lower the population of feral cats in the park. With all the natural dangers that stalk them, the birds don't need the additional predation by cats—estimates of birds killed by cats run in the millions—and the cats she's able to place in homes live longer, healthier lives. During one recent summer, she captured 50 feral cats in Latodami—and many of them were pregnant. By the end of the summer, she had found homes for 100 of the cats and their offspring. Unfortunately, she couldn't find homes for all of them.

(One of her alumni is trying to catch the cursor as I type.)

Joe Grom's stream is flowing again. In June, its loud chatter was pleasing, but not surprising. It was just another of the happy background woodland sounds. It's hardly chattering now, but if I'm very still, I can hear it gurgle softly. After three mute months, that whisper makes me want to leap into a pool and stamp and splash with joy. And who would know, or laugh at me? Nobody, of course, but it would disturb the water striders, and they've had troubles enough. That they are here, skating these little pools after the long drought, seems a miracle. Where do they go when the water goes away? Surely they can't walk the dry rocks to the waters down the hill. Those airy feet are meant to stride the insubstantial: an invisible film laid between two worlds and built of nothing more than the asymmetric attractions among molecules. Yet here they are: beyond the drought and walking nonchalantly on a theory.

The water they tread is on loan from the Gulf of Mexico. We'll pass it through uncounted creatures, large and small, and return it.

We do get used to some very strange ideas.

October

Merlin's Trees

Like the wick within the flame,
they stand inside October's fire:
the pillars of obsidian that gleam
beneath a scarlet canopy
in the brilliance after rain.

I think that, when their songs
fly southward with the sun,
these earthbound ones who must remain,
find in alchemy, new art:
weave, from first frost, spells of radiance:
They vanish under shimmering veils
of orange fire and yellow haze,
march down the awestruck hills
as sun gods robed in gleaming gold.

Bedazzled, I just stand and blink
through tears of ecstasy and anguish.
For the magic fades as nights grow long.
A sudden breath of northern air
foretells November gales they cannot face
arrayed in gossamer and gauze.
So one wild night, they'll rub
their twiggy fingers on the wind,
shed their summer skins
in swirling clouds of glitter,
and loom against a low gray sky,
stark and black and skeletal.
And I will grieve and kick dry leaves,
head bowed, and pass unseeing
through a grove of gnarled sorcerers
who stand, ankle-deep in yesterday,
tomorrows safely sown,
and pondering, as first snow flies,
the shape of May's enchantment.

October 3

And now a year has passed. I find myself standing under the hardwoods by
Grom Run on a warm, misty morning with the heaviness in my chest that
farewells bring. That's odd. This is to be the last entry, but the woods show no
inclination to leave, and I'm surely coming back. Odd.

The woods seem moody, too: damp, subdued, heavy. Hurricane Lili is raging
ashore in Louisiana, but there isn't a breath of wind here. We wait. Some of the
rain we need is forecast for tonight. Perhaps Lili will bring the rest tomorrow.

Even the flock of small birds is subdued. Chickadees, Carolina wrens,
nuthatches, and a pair of downy woodpeckers pass through, but without their
usual boisterousness. Yellow leaves tumble among them. A quick glance asks,
"Warblers?" But no. They've probably flown south. I hope they're not flying
into Lili. They've become family.

The mood changes abruptly. The hillside cheeps, whirs, and chatters with the
alarms of birds and squirrels. Some hunter creeps among the barberries, but I
can't see it. Jays, towhees, flickers, titmice and wrens can, though. Their fervor
surprises me a bit. The hunter is on foot. It can't catch them. Their nests have
been empty for months. Why the furor? Theory says that scolding is a way to
teach the young what to fear. Indeed, deer stroll the woods without a glance
from the birds. The gray cat and its ilk, on the other hand, have probably earned,
and certainly get, an escort of loud, angry birds. I don't know what predator is
giving the object lesson today.

Whatever it was has passed, and squirrels, chipmunks, and birds are about their
usual business. Loud hooting from a large walnut tree surprises me, but the birds
and beasts seem unconcerned. The barred owl! The thought and the owl pass
swiftly and simultaneously, one through and the other right over my head. One
jay swims in the owl's wake, screaming.

The stream still flows, but meagerly again. The patch of snakeroot that
supplanted the bee balm is, itself, now ragged and chewed. The white flowers
have turned brown; the leaves are beginning to yellow. Next in the succession
is—snow? But not soon. It's still easy to find salamanders under the rocks.
Most are northern dusky salamanders, but one is brown with two lines of spots.
The color and pattern remind me of a trout. It moves as quickly, too. Too
quickly for a novice to identify.

The next leg of my farewell tour leads up the hill to the windmill in the meadow.
A south wind is strengthening. The sky is still gray. Several birds are active. A

towhee, a cardinal, a song sparrow, a small flock of goldfinches, and a couple of sparrows I can't identify flit through the American bittersweet that covers the windmill and much of the apple tree. Suddenly, their calls are different than any I've ever heard, and before I can blink, I'm staring into the yellow eyes of a sharp-shinned hawk. It's perched on a large limb of the apple tree about six feet away! We're both surprised, but it doesn't seem frightened. It just looks into my eyes for a long second, then vanishes, to re-materialize in the air outside the tree. It perches for a while in a nearby cherry tree, then floats swiftly along the meadow's edge and out of sight.

I'm left inspecting the tree for paths in and out of the tangle of apple and bittersweet branches. There simply aren't any. Yet the hawk flew in and back out without touching a leaf or making a sound while moving faster than my eyes could follow. I had read that sharp-shinned hawks can fly, at full speed, through a bush without touching it. Until now, I thought that was an exaggeration. Perhaps the odd birdcalls I heard were their equivalent of the bullfrogs' groans.

For a while, the little copse is quiet. Or maybe I'm just busy digesting that experience. The last leg of my tour calls, but as I'm about to walk into the open, the white rump and long tail of a northern harrier flash by near the line of bushes that bisects the meadow. It, too, vanishes into the woods.

The leaves of the dogwoods of May are turning red. Most of their bright red berries are gone, but uncountable silver buds dream of spring. And so down the hill to the pond.

The moss-covered log where the skimmers laid their eggs last year is currently occupied by several small green frogs. But otherwise, the pond reminds me of a book, <u>The Strange Life of Ivan Osokin</u>. The first and third-to-the-last chapters of that book are absolutely identical. Life repeats itself—almost. And so is the pond so very like it was last October 3. Breezes ruffle water whose level is slightly lower—this year, no water flows into the stream below. Only three mallards paddle about on the opposite side. The large green-striped dragonflies patrol their domains. Two phoebes flick their tails as they peer this way and that from bare branches of overhanging trees. And a kingfisher rattles by. So very familiar. So very much the same. And as before, some will soon fly south, some dive deep into the mud. Some have laid, already, their plans for May in secret spots I won't likely visit. Yet these dragonflies, frogs, and phoebes may well not be the same ones that I met last fall. Even more certainly, those that return to— or reemerge into—their ancestral home next spring will be the children or the children's children of last year's class. I hope to be here, too, to greet them. But one day, their progeny will be greeted by some of those boisterous youngsters that Meg Scanlon and the teachers led around the pond this summer. I find immense satisfaction in that.

> *Next year, and next again,*
> *will find new singers,*
> *new listeners on the shore,*
> *but the old, old songs*
> *and the ancient joy.*

174

And Finally

So, what have I learned from this pew in the woods as it traveled round the sun? That is a very long journey, after all. What have I to show for it? What beyond the obvious: days spent wandering in loveliness, new names for things, new awareness, a lot of stories and a poem or two, some tattered leaves pressed in books? Are these all? Are these enough?

Well, why does anyone sit in any pew? I think we sit us down to find, or reaffirm, our place in this whirl of infinities: time and space beyond imagining, fates and forces far beyond our strengths, complexities beyond unraveling. Some of us sit in one pew all our lives; some hop from pew to pew until we find the one that fits—or maybe we outgrow them. I'm surely of the latter group. And from this pew, I saw one more infinity: the tapestry of intertwining fates that builds even such a little woodland. Its threads stretch from the warblers of Brazil to the juncoes of Canada. Waters from the Gulf near Yucatan flow down Grom Run. The snow that didn't fall last winter was lost to centuries of industry; their oxides flow in every breeze. This woodland is, indeed, one of the grains of sand that one can see the universe within.

I conceded long ago that comprehending such things whole is quite beyond me. Whatever Finger stirs the galaxies, the solar system, and the molecules within our cells must be larger than our minds can wrap around. Yet I still can't leave it be.

So this pilgrimage into the woods. To the woods to see firsthand that Finger stirring one full cycle around the sun, to watch the flow as closely as I can. And as I leave these woods, I carry my lesson. Although the tapestry stretches out of sight in all directions, I can see enough of God to live by in the details: in the heroism of parenthood and the cold eyes of the hunt, in the nest and in the spider's web. The beauty and the savagery, the joy and the despair, are woven into something wondrous. It's enough to turn a chemist mystical. When I consider the colors of the pond in late October, the tanager amidst dogwood blossoms, all those parents—furred or feathered—and their trials, spider webs and midges glistening in the sun …it's all that I can do to keep from stumbling into poetry. Indeed, I do keep tumbling in.

One thing more. I find I'm carrying, once again, the love of a place and the pains of that love. North Park is a true microcosm that reflects the pressures of growth upon all things non-human. Housing developments lean against its edges. Trucks rumble down the road that bisects the nature center. It is even threatened by those whose job is to protect it. Those surrounding developments have sent acres of silt into North Park Lake. The county's leaders have pledged to restore the lake, but where to put the silt? The Army Corps of Engineers has proposed that it be dumped onto the upper meadow of Latodami—thirty acres of mud, thirty feet deep! As I write, that proposal is still a possibility. But it is no longer a certainty. Public opposition may still protect Latodami. A number of us are urging the county leadership to find another, hopefully constructive solution, and we have been heard.

The lesson is an old one: since Latodami's inhabitants neither pay taxes nor vote, their voices only reach the higher echelons of leadership if we speak for them. So we must speak.

In my darker moments, I fear that they will lose, not this battle, perhaps, but the larger conflict. Unless we can control our numbers and our appetites, I think it is inevitable that we humans will destroy much we need and love in our march across the planet. One day, we will unleash something much larger than ourselves. Perhaps we have already. And on the day we realize what we've done, we will also realize that our fate is tied inextricably to the fates of all of the planet's other inhabitants. If our species does survive itself, as it may, since *Homo Sapiens* is so very adaptable, it will have had to change, probably beyond our recognition. I'm unlikely to be there to know. It's unlikely I'd want to be.

The natural world will change as well and carry on, with or without us. Two years ago, after a heavy January snowfall, I wandered the woods by Walter Road wondering where the ground feeding birds could find food. I found neither open ground nor birds in the woods. In the parking lot, though, a flock of juncoes pecked among the weeds that poked up through the fissures in the asphalt. So it goes now, and so it will go as some calamity we've nurtured bears down on us and all else that lives upon the world: some stoic and adaptive few will find a living among the cracks in our civilization. As the cracks grow wider, they will thrive, and in ten million years, who will know or care that we were here? There will be new beauty and new eyes to wonder at the miracle.

I find solace in knowing this. Calamities far greater than humanity have fallen upon the world—quite literally. At least two massive meteors have torn huge sections from the tapestry of life and, each time, the tapestry has woven itself anew into another as beautiful and more intricate than the last. The first meteor led to the dinosaurs' world, the second to ours. We are, despite our hubris, only small lips sipping from the surge of life.

My despair then, when I succumb to it, is not for the world, but for this world: the thrush's fluting in May, the rain of golden leaves in autumn. But, as any thrush could testify, despair will not get you from Yucatan to Pittsburgh when the north wind's in your face. Better, he'd say, to leap joyfully into the night and fly with every ounce of strength to where your heart commands.

Mine sent me to a little urban woodland, to meetings to preserve it, and to this keyboard to record my wanderings there. I hope you'll be inspired to find your Latodami and the universe within it. You'll have to be still, but you won't have to go very far.